DAVID POULSEN
Don't Fence Me In

David Poulsen has been an actor, rock singer, college English Instructor and high school football coach. For the past 20 years, he has traveled the rodeo circuit, first as a bareback rider, then as a rodeo clown, and most recently as a broadcaster/commentator for many of Canada's biggest rodeos including the Calgary Stampede and the Canadian Finals Rodeo. His literary career began in earnest when his story "The Welcomin'" won the Alberta Culture Short Story Writing Competition. His previous books include a trilogy for young adults—*The Cowboy Kid, Ride for the Crown,* and *Ride the High Country*—and a collection of stories called *Dream.* David Poulsen lives in the rolling foothills southwest of Calgary, Alberta.

For Diana —

DON'T FENCE ME IN

ME IN

A ROMANCE OF THE NEW WEST

✳ **David Poulsen** ✳

My best to you !!

David

Red Deer College Press

THE PUBLISHERS
Red Deer College Press
56 Avenue & 32 Street Box 5005
Red Deer Alberta Canada T4N 5H5

CREDITS
Cover Art and Design by Kurt Hafso
Text Design by Dennis Johnson
Printed & Bound in Canada by Parkland ColourPress Ltd.
for Red Deer College Press
Special thanks to Dawn Stolz, Jim Beckel and G & H Harley
Davidson for their assistance in preparation of this book

ACKNOWLEDGEMENTS
Financial support provided by the Alberta Foundation for the Arts, a beneficiary of the Lottery Fund of the Government of Alberta, and by the Canada Council, the Department of Communications and Red Deer College.

The stories "Ralph the Dog – A Love Story" and "Midnight" previously appeared in different form in the collection *Dream*, Plains Publishing, 1990.

The Alberta
Foundation
for the Arts

Providing a foundation for the arts

THE SOURCE
OF MANY BENEFITS

CANADIAN CATALOGUING IN PUBLICATION DATA
Poulsen, David A. 1946–
Don't fence me in
ISBN 0-88995-109-8
I. Title.
PS8581.O848D6 1993 C813'.54 C93-091492-9
PR9199.3.P68D6 1993

To L. A.

Just turn me lose,
Let me straddle my old saddle underneath the western skies.
On my cayuse,
Let me wonder over yonder til I see the mountains rise.
I want to ride to the ridge where the west commences,
Gaze at the moon til I lose my senses,
Can't look at hobbles and I can't stand fences,
Don't fence me in.

—COLE PORTER

PROLOGUE

Cause and effect, that's what it all boils down to. Something happens, which causes something else to happen, then something else and so on.

I almost get killed by a bull, and while I'm recovering in the hospital, my dad comes by for a visit and leaves a couple of tickets for a football game. I go to the game and fall in love with the home team's mascot. Sadly, the mascot doesn't feel the same as I do. Then they make a movie of my dad's life as a former rodeo great, and as for the mascot and me, well I guess that's what this is all about. But it all makes sense, no kidding. It's just cause and effect.

I'm a forty-one-year-old, mostly unemployed rodeo clown. I've been looking at bulls who've been looking back at me for twenty-two years. The tangible rewards of this activity have been few. Damn few. I drive a '62 GMC pickup with one rusted-out fender and an unfixable knock in the transmission. I own three pairs of jeans, five shirts, two of them identical, a not-bad selection of underwear and socks, a quarter section of bottomland in Saskatchewan, thirty or forty cassettes, mostly rock, and a complete set of Val d'Or china, including the creamer and gravy boat. The latter came into my possession only indirectly through rodeo. I got drunk at a rodeo dance in Gillette, Wyoming, and bought seventy-five bucks worth of raffle tickets on a Jeep Cherokee. I didn't win the Jeep. The dishes were second prize, but it could've been worse. Third prize was a three-year supply of panty hose.

There are times when I'm convinced I'm the reincarnation of the western outlaw, Doc Holliday. I also have this thing for Mary Steenburgen. I've seen all her movies, some of them often enough to have memorized all of her dialogue. I figure you really must care about someone to sit through *Back to the Future III* seventeen times.

There's something else. I occasionally see things before they happen. I guess that makes me psychic or clairvoyant or something. Like Edgar Cayce. Some people would find that interesting, but not everyone. In fact, a number of people, notably my ex-wife and son, have concluded that I am clinically, though not dangerously, insane.

Truth is, I want to be a writer. At a time when the publishing business is at a low point, when governments treat artists like carriers of contagious diseases and Canadians read American books in record numbers, I want to be a writer.

That's the good stuff about me.

There's also some shit happening in my life.

CHAPTER ONE

The voice of rodeo announcer Dick Leatherbee prattled on endlessly. Normally, I don't hear the words, just an irritating drone like the noise mosquitoes make to keep you awake in a dark tent.

Leatherbee never actually shuts up so the voice is always there, but I'm usually concentrating on more important things. Which is what I should have been doing at that particular moment because standing a short distance from me was a cross-bred Brahma bull named Richter Scale. And it was clear from his body language and certain graceless noises he was making that Richter Scale wasn't fond of me. Which should have been all the incentive I needed to focus a hundred percent on him.

Nevertheless, Leatherbee's babble continued to sandpaper its way into my consciousness.

"And now watch this, folks. The man in the funny clothes with a serious job to do, rodeo clown Doc Allen, is about to show you why he's considered one of the best in the business."

One thing I'm sure of, it wasn't vanity that made me hear the words that day. I was perfectly aware that Dick Leatherbee offered up the same platitudes at exactly the same point of every rodeo performance he worked no matter who the clown happened to be.

I tried to push the announcer's voice out of my mind and refocus on Richter Scale, who was becoming increasingly impatient with the fact that he and I shared the same planet. He continued to make an assortment of snorts and under-his-breath grunts. Then the grunts became fewer and the snorts more frequent, and while I don't consider myself an expert in the language of bovines, I was pretty sure Richter Scale was warning me for the last time.

People often ask what goes through my mind as I stand nose to nose with an animal whose sole purpose in life appears to be separating my body parts. It's a favorite query of people in the media, for example, just before they ask the inevitable, "Ever been hurt?" and then, "Yeah? How bad?"

What goes through my mind I figure is mostly air. In other words, I don't think about it a lot. It's what I do, that's all. Some people sell cars; some fill cavities; I fight bulls. And most of the time, I like the job, but Richter Scale wasn't like most bulls.

Maybe I lied when I said I don't think about what I do. I have to admit that as I get older and the bulls get meaner, and faster, I've started examining some of the more metaphysical aspects of rodeo clowning. Which perhaps explains why, as Richter Scale began his charge, there was a thought running through my head. But it had nothing to do with Leatherbee's BS about showing them why I'm considered one of the best in the business. No, the thought was more of the "Only a dickhead would do this" variety.

Richter Scale is what's called a fighting bull in rodeo parlance. He rarely gets bucked in the performance but is sent out for the clowns to "play with" for the enjoyment of the crowd. This bull seemed uninterested in things metaphysical. He lowered his head a bit, I assumed to increase the trajectory of my impending flight through the air.

I gave him the old "feint left, dodge right" maneuver that had worked a thousand times before. Unfortunately, Richter Scale was familiar with this particular move and wasn't even slightly fooled. His left horn, a protuberance of considerable proportion, grazed my left thigh. It's important to understand that even a graze from the horn of a bull moving at top speed can mean hospitalization for the grazee. I stumbled slightly, recovered and turned to face the bull, who had also turned and was lining me up for another pass.

I recently read an article by an animal rights activist who opposed rodeo, in part because clowns humiliate bulls during bull riding events. I can't honestly say I could see much humiliation in ol' Richter Scale as he drew a bead on me. He was upset, no doubt, maybe even pissed off, but embarrassed? I don't think so.

The clown barrel was about thirty feet away, and from the corner of my eye I caught a glimpse of Tub Willoughby leaning out of the barrel, waving and hollering like crazy to get the bull's attention. Tub's a veteran barrel man and knows when a bullfighter is in trouble. Unfortunately, Richter Scale didn't give a rip about Tub; he only had eyes for me, as the popular song, probably written for different circumstances, goes.

When evading a bull, the idea is to keep moving in small circles. A bull can easily outrun a man but isn't able to turn quickly, so if you circle him a few times, eventually he gives up and lopes off to check out the heifers in a pen at the other end of the arena. That's the theory. But this particular bull—he was now eyeing me from about three meters away and pawing the ground—clearly wasn't well-versed with the theory.

He eyed and pawed some more, so I got down and eyed and pawed, too. This is a moment that rodeo fans love, the clown on all fours, eyeball to eyeball with the bull, both flinging dirt behind them.

While the crowd finds this hilarious, it can be dangerous in the extreme for the clown. It takes a second or two to regain your feet, and if you slip even slightly, the result is almost sure to involve people in the medical profession.

So why was a guy like me, who's been in this business long enough to know better, bothering with the pawing the dirt bit? I didn't even do that shit as a young up-and-coming bullfighter, eager to impress rodeo committees who did the hiring. Well, maybe I did once or twice. Anyway, I'm an old bullfighter now, and I've learned a few things. It took me years to figure out that, like a lot of things, success in rodeo is mostly based on who you know, that committees are as loyal as California hookers and that if you get maimed pulling crap like what I was doing at that exact moment, it didn't matter if they wanted to hire you because you couldn't work anyway.

So I figure it had to be Dad. My dad hadn't seen me work more than three or four times in my entire career and not at all in the last seven or eight years. But he was here today, somewhere behind the chutes, watching me. Or more likely, knowing Dad, he was wandering through the crowd conducting a comparative study of halter tops and their contents.

It occurred to me that if I wanted to see my father or anyone else ever again, I'd better get up off my hands and knees and make a serious move for Tub's barrel. I was just back to my feet when the bull charged. I'd been saving one more move, and I figured the time was about right.

It's kind of a spinnerama maneuver, which, if it works, is a thing of beauty. What isn't so hot about it is I have to turn my back completely on the bull, which tends to leave one "exposed" as we in the trade say.

I should have realized I was in trouble when Richter Scale slowed down. As a bullfighter I like to see the bull going full speed, head down, not really thinking about what he's doing. But Richter Scale was thinking. And the spinnerama move fooled him even less than the "feint left, dodge right." I first realized this when I felt the jab of a horn. I'm not sure if it was the left or right this time as it took place during the "exposed" phase of the spinnerama. What his horn jabbed was my backside, specifically that part of my backside involved in a bodily function not talked about in polite society.

So I won't, but I can tell you it hurt to beat hell. Not that I had a lot of time to think about pain as I flailed my way through the air. Which brings us back to the humiliation issue. Fact is, I was becoming more embarrassed all the time by what was going on out there.

The only good thing about the situation was that Richter Scale had flung me . . . butted me . . . projected me, any number of verbs would work here, in the direction of Tub Willoughby and the sanctuary offered by his crimson barrel.

My landing had none of the precision of space shuttles, but I was able to scramble up and duck behind the barrel just as Richter Scale roared by, intent on seeing a repeat performance of my attempted mastery of flight. Then he trotted away, apparently content with his afternoon's accomplishments.

"It's okay, Tub. You can come up now," I said.

"You okay?" he asked, popping his head up out of the barrel. "He gave you a pretty good lick."

"Yeah, I'm all right," I said, leaning on the barrel and trying to wave to the crowd, who obviously found the whole sequence pretty damn funny.

Stock contractor Stan Shofner rode over on his big bald-faced sorrel horse and said, "Hey, clown, work him some more. They like it."

I hate it when people call me "clown."

"Work him yourself, Stan," I said between attempts to replenish my oxygen supply. "I gave them their money's worth."

"Chickenshit," Stan said and rode off to tell the guy on the gate to let the bull out.

I like "chickenshit" even less than "clown."

"He's a sweetheart, ol' Stan," said Tub while climbing out of the barrel.

"He's an asshole."

"You always did have a better vocabulary than me," Tub grinned as we started for the chutes.

The fighting bull is the last event at a rodeo so Dick Leatherbee was wrapping things up on the microphone and saying goodbye to the paying customers as we made our way out of the arena.

"You sure you're okay?" Tub asked again. "You're walking like he shoved a horn up your ass."

"Naw, just pulled a hamstring a little is all." I was searching the faces behind the chutes for Dad.

He was right there behind chute six, and I was looking forward to hearing what he had to say. I mean, what the hell, I'd had a pretty good day out there. As we got closer, I smiled my victory smile and tried not to walk like I hurt. But some pain is harder to hide, like what I was feeling at that moment.

My father glared at me. "It's Tuesday, goddammit!"

They weren't exactly the words I'd expected to hear.

"Yes, Dad," I nodded, "I know what day it is."

CHAPTER TWO

In his day my father had been maybe the best rodeo clown ever to wear the makeup and baggy pants. At least that's the way I had it figured when I was growing up. To tell the truth, I probably still feel that way.

Dad, who called himself "Hoot" in his clownin' days, was from the old school. Meaning that he performed both rodeo clown roles—the bullfighter, which is about protecting cowboys during and after bull rides, and funnyman, which is about amusing the crowd.

Nowadays there's specialists. There's bullfighters, who are often funny in the same way colitis is funny, and there's barrel men, some of whom are scared to death of creatures with four legs but who can make people in the grandstands laugh to beat hell.

Dad got me started in the business when I was about three. He had an act called "The Shrinking Clown Routine." He'd roll his clown barrel into the arena and then start bragging to the announcer about how brave he was. Eventually the announcer'd yell, "Look out! There's a bull loose in the arena!" and Hoot, he'd jump into the barrel and crouch down out of sight like he was scared to death.

Then some cowboy who was in on the routine would come over to the barrel, look inside and say something to the announcer like, "Oh, you shouldn't a done that. Ya skeered 'im so bad he's shrunk." Honest, that's how they talked—ya skeered 'im.

Of course, I was inside the barrel dressed exactly like Dad, except in miniature, and up I'd pop. The crowd would go nuts.

Which maybe tells you something about rodeo crowds.

I kind of liked it. Partly because I got to do something with my dad and partly because I liked the attention of an audience. I figured out early that rodeo could give me a self-esteem upper, and I've been at it ever since. Once I got too old for the shrinking clown routine, I graduated to riding steers and then broncs. I was lousy at both, but by then the whole cowboy mystique was as much a part of my being as my belly-button, so it seemed logical to follow in Hoot's footsteps or, more accurately, cleat marks.

One thing Dad always said to me or anybody else who'd listen was don't ever fight bulls on a Tuesday. And if you were ever stupid enough to ask him why not, which I was on more than one occasion, then you'd hear the whole litany of Dad's "horror on Tuesday" stories.

There was Tuesday, July 6, 1951, at the Calgary Stampede when a bull named Wall Street got a horn stuck in Dad's suspenders and shook him up and down like a kid shakin' a piggy bank. That one resulted in a three-week stay in a hospital located conveniently near the Stampede grounds.

Then came a Tuesday in 1957, at San Antone, when a critter with the unlikely name of Saturday Matinee went past Dad and then kicked out behind, catching him right on the point of his chin and causing an interesting repositioning of brain cells that rendered him unconscious for about five minutes. He was back, though sporting a couple of stitches, for the next performance.

That was followed by Tuesday, December 8—I think it was 1960 or so—at Oklahoma City, when Dad was trying to untie a bull rider hung up in his bull rope. Dad got stepped on by the bull, had three ribs crushed and a lung punctured, and missed out on a date with Barbara Ann Scott, the figure skater.

It was some newspaper promotion deal. Of course, they were both married to someone else by then, but Dad told me later he was prepared to dump Mom for Barbara Ann if the situation looked promising. Strictly for genetic reasons, he'd said. And if you think about it, crossing a figure skater with a rodeo clown, combining the athleticism and the grace of one with the dash and daring of the other, could have revolutionized rodeo clowning . . . and maybe figure skating, too.

Like I said, the date thing never came off so Dad and Mom stayed together, and the only cross they ever got was me. And I'd just finished fighting bulls in Cloverdale, British Columbia, on a Tuesday, and Dad was pissed off.

"Goddammit, it's Tuesday," he said again.

"Yeah, Dad, I know."

I'd taken Dad to Cloverdale with me because I figured he needed to get out and around more. When Mom died nine years earlier, Dad quit going to rodeos, quit working on his old car, a '52 de Soto he'd been restoring for about eleven years, and he'd even packed away his crib board, a sure sign that he'd given up and was merely waiting around to die. Except that he didn't. Instead, he got more bored and more crotchety and spent most of his time bitching about the aging process and reminding anyone within earshot that he was only minutes away from his final reward. "I never buy green bananas because I can't be sure I'll be around long enough to see 'em ripen," he told me once.

I'd tried other forms of diversion with less than spectacular results. Fishing, tickets to hockey games and signing him up for handicraft classes at the local community center had been greeted with groans, curses and other less formal verbalizations.

This time, my thinking was, if he was in Cloverdale with me, at least it would get him thinking about something other than the fact that he was old. Even if the thinking had to do with what a jerk his son was.

"And your spinnerama was horseshit," he barked.

I'd forgotten he'd taught it to me.

"I slipped," I told him.

"Don't give me that crap."

"Want something to eat?" I changed the subject as we walked toward the motor home I'd rented for most of what I'd earn at Cloverdale.

"How many times have I told you about fighting bulls on Tuesdays?" He was staring straight ahead to show me how mad he was.

"Quite a few times, Dad."

"Well, why do you do it then?"

"Because the committee refuses to cancel the rodeo when they've got a beautiful day and a full grandstand just because the clown's father thinks it's a good idea."

Dad didn't say anything for a second, but he scuffed the dirt a couple of times.

"Why you walkin' like that?" he growled. "He shove a horn up your ass?"

"Naw." I lied for the second time in five minutes. "A little hamstring pull, that's all."

"Hi boys. Nice job, Doc."

The voice belonged to Rhonda Rae Crockett, gorgeous, about twenty-six, maybe twenty-seven. She was one of those barrel racers who competed at about a hundred rodeos a year and never won a dime.

I figured she was either independently wealthy or had a sugar daddy somewhere because paying entry fees in order to lose never seemed to bother her. In fact, most of the time when you saw her, she was smiling. She was smiling now as she passed in front of us with her traveling partner, Lane Huxley, another barrel racer. Lane won more than Rhonda Rae but smiled less, an odd contradiction if you ask me.

I detoured Dad away from the motor home and over to a big tent where the rodeo committee treated the cowboys to a beer and something to eat. I sat Dad down at a picnic table with a beef on a bun and went to get us a couple of drinks.

When I came back, Dad said, "She's giving me the eye."

"Who?" I looked in the direction he was waving his fork and saw Rhonda Rae surrounded by a bunch of American bulldoggers, the smallest of whom was the size of a hotel.

"Think I should give her a tumble?" Dad looked at me.

"You're sixty-three years old," I told him, and I knew right away it was the wrong thing to say.

"What the hell do you call this?" He held up the glass of Coke I'd brought him and screwed up his face like it was a urine sample.

"It's too early for beer." I was starting to think that four more days at Cloverdale with Hoot could get stressful.

After we finished eating, it took considerable effort to get Dad out of the beer tent and away from Rhonda Rae. When he finally settled down, we had a reasonably quiet evening playing gin rummy and talking about the internal politics of rodeo, which as near as I can figure follows the example of the United Church. In other words, rodeo operates on the premise that chaos and strife are good things. Then we read for a while before bed.

I was re-reading *The Drifters* and thinking wistfully of Spain. Occasionally, I looked over at Dad, who was thumbing the pages of an old *Vancouver Sun* he'd found in a closet.

Physically, there wasn't a lot of similarity between us. I'm taller by about three inches and have a slighter build. My hair is long and light brown; his is cropped short and dark brown, except for the grey, of course. He has a big chest, long arms and is clean shaven. I have a substantial—it sounds better than big—ass, long legs and a moustache. Oh yeah, and his eyes are an intense dark brown. Mine are blue. I've sometimes wondered if we're really related.

We also differ when it comes to reading. Dad doesn't believe in it. He tries, whenever possible, to include the word "wimp" in every sentence that contains the word "read."

After several minutes of what was for him intense perusal, he put the paper down and announced that Brian Mulroney was a Communist. My own knowledge of politics is sketchy, but I was fairly sure that the one, and maybe the only, unpleasant label one could not attach to the Prime Minister was that of Communist.

Of course, Hoot was from the old school, the one that said the worst thing you could say about somebody was that he was a Communist, and Dad was searching for the worst thing he could say about Mulroney—in itself, not an altogether unworthy sentiment.

I thought about trying to explain Communism to Dad, then remembered that I'd gone through it before—Marx, the Manifesto, all of it. At the end of the discussion, he'd stood up, belched and said, "Yeah, well as far as I'm concerned, the Edmonton Oilers are all fucking Communists."

So this time I just nodded and turned the page of my book.

Not long afterward, Dad suggested we check out the peelers. I was half an hour convincing him that sleep was a viable alternative.

The next morning I woke to discover that Dad was already up and gone from the motor home. I lay there for a few minutes staring at a couple of poorly done welds in the ceiling and asking myself how much trouble the old guy could get into.

As possible answers began filtering through the morning fog encasing my brain, I got up and dressed in a hurry. I found Dad a couple of motor homes down, drinking coffee and visiting with an older couple. Well, older than me, younger than him. As I approached, Dad turned in his lawn chair and pointed at me.

"That's him now."

I hoped he wasn't going to embarrass me with a bunch of his this-is-the-terrific-kid-I've-been-telling-you-about stuff.

"That's him," Dad said again. "That's the son-of-a-bitch that fights bulls on Tuesdays."

I should've known better. Come to think of it, I can't actually remember my dad ever being guilty of the terrific-kid thing anyway.

"Feel like breakfast?" I asked him.

"Had 'er." He turned back to the man and woman. "The . . . what'd you say your names was? . . ."

"The Claysmores . . . the Claysmores," the man said in that loud voice people use when they think everybody over sixty is deaf.

"The Claysmores here fed me just fine," Dad continued. "We had cereal and fruit and . . . they were some kind of eggs, weren't they?"

"Yes, they were," Mrs. Claysmore nodded and managed to keep a sort of half smile pasted on her face, although I had the feeling she'd had happier mornings.

"Say hello to Phil and Doris," Dad completed the introduction.

"Roy and June," Mr. Claysmore amended and regarded me with a look that clearly said, Please rescue us from this erratic person for whom you are responsible.

I ignored the look and glanced at my watch. It was just after eight. I figured the concession that served up pancake breakfast ought to be in full operation.

"Well, maybe I'll go get myself a little sustenance." I smiled at the three of them. "Gee, Dad, you should tell these nice folks about some of the problems you've encountered on Tuesdays. See ya."

I headed off, not hating myself that much, knowing that Dad and the Claysmores would be talking for at least another hour. What the hell. It wasn't that different from plunking a kid down to watch cartoons.

"Hey!" Dad's voice had a note of adolescent urgency to it as he stuck his head in the door of the motor home. "C'mon. You don't wanna miss this."

I was applying a tear, part of my clown makeup, and didn't feel like being disturbed for any of Dad's silliness.

"What's up?" I swiveled around in the chair to look at him.

"Come on, come on, hurry up!" He was gesturing a lot and looking over his shoulder, and his face was flushed. I considered ignoring him on the off chance that he might go away.

He didn't, so because he's my father and because our Judaeo-Christian tradition says that counts for something, I reluctantly set the tube of Clown White back in my fishing-tackle-box-cum-makeup-kit and pulled on a shirt as I followed Dad out of the trailer.

"What's going on?" I looked at him as he tugged at my arm and hauled me toward the chutes.

"Num–ber . . . four." He had begun to giggle and was having trouble talking.

Somebody came out of chute number one on a saddle bronc and was bucked off just about the time Dad and I arrived at the front of chute four.

"From Helena, Montana, the next cowboy is Clark Heskie," Dick Leatherbee's voice crackled over the loudspeaker. The crackling wasn't the sound system's fault. That was Leatherbee's normal voice.

"Clark's a veteran of the rodeo trail . . . been gettin' on saddle broncs for thirteen seasons now," he informed the crowd.

What Leatherbee was saying was perfectly true. What he didn't say was that Clark Heskie's intellectual powers were roughly equivalent to those of a post pounder. He was perched above the horse now, one leg on each side of the chute, and Stan Shofner was up there, too, ready to tighten the flank strap when the gate opened.

Suddenly, the energy level of the whole scene increased dramatically. A soggy bellow issued from Stan Shofner's chewing tobacco crammed mouth, which I interpreted as, "Whadda fuck happened tuh my horse's tail?"

At about that moment, my father had drifted to a position behind me and was hunkered down, giggling harder now and covering his mouth with his hand. Clark Heskie, that thirteen-year veteran of the rodeo trail, found himself jerked from the saddle and brought nose to nose with a very upset Stan Shofner.

"Whadda fuck didja do tuh my horse?"

Stan Shofner stands about six-four in stocking feet and Clark might make five-seven on his tippy toes, so for them to be nose to nose, either Stan has to bend down or Clark has to be off the ground quite a ways.

Stan was not bending down.

In the flurry of body shaking, profanities and explanations that followed, I was just able pick out Clark's feeble voice.

"But your assistant told me to. He said the horse bucks better with his tail trimmed. He told me you wouldn't mind."

"What assistant, you dumb fuck?"

I detected a recurring pattern in Stan's vocabulary.

"That little old guy that works for you." Clark was having a lot of trouble speaking clearly because a lot of his shirt and all ten of Stan's knuckles were wedged under his chin

Stan, on the other hand, was most effective in articulating his anger. In fact, most of the crowd in the main grandstand was enjoying the behind-the-scenes drama that had brought the rodeo to a grinding halt.

"You'll pay, you son-of-a-bitch." At last Stan had varied his word choice.

"Sure, Stan, sure."

"Big time!"

"Sure, Stan, sure."

"Five hundred bucks!"

"Five hundred? But—"

"Five hundred or I throw you down in that chute and let this horse dance on your goddamn face."

"Five hundred. Sure, Stan, sure," said Clark Heskie, suddenly finding the amount quite reasonable.

I turned to admonish my sixty-three-year-old kid of a father, but in all the excitement, he had made good his escape. I did the same. I caught up with him on the way back to the motor home. He was staggering back and forth and wheezing so hard that my first thought was heart attack.

"That was dumb, Dad." I patted him on the back, hard.

"You think I'm dumb?" Dad hiccuped out the words between guffaws. "Not as dumb as that bronc rider. At least I never paid five hundred bucks for a piece of tail."

The punch line was even dumber than the joke, but as I went into the motor home, Dad stumbled off in the direction of the concession stand, no doubt to repeat it a couple dozen more times.

CHAPTER THREE

The bull riding segment of the second rodeo performance at Cloverdale was going along about as well as could be expected considering my ass hurt everytime I took a step.

And I'd have gotten through it, except that Ty Decker's bull didn't buck a jump, which meant he got a re-ride, and the re-ride bull was Richter Scale.

Stan Shofner rode by and said, "I guess we'll find out what you're made of now, chickenshit."

"You know, Stan, you used to be a pretty good guy till you started spending your nights with Brahma heifers," I told him.

"Fuck you," Stan said and rode off.

"I'll never beat a comeback like that," I said to Tub.

"Okay, get serious now. Don't jack with this puppy," Tub said as we both stared at chute four where Decker was getting down on Richter Scale. "He could eat your lunch."

"I hear ya." I stepped away from the barrel and took up my spot in front of the chute gate.

I was focusing harder on the bull than I was on Ty Decker, and as Richter Scale turned his head and looked out at me—maybe it was just my imagination—I could've sworn he was grinning.

Ty Decker wasn't the guy I would have picked to be on this bull. Decker got hung up in his rope more than normal, and if he got hung up on Richter Scale, things could get real ugly for all of us, except maybe the bull.

The gate opened and for a bull as nasty as he was, Richter Scale wasn't a great bucker. But he stumbled and that was enough to get Decker in trouble. The next thing I knew, he was bucked off. Except for his hand, which was still tied into his bull rope, which was still securely attached to the back of Richter Scale.

"Stay on your feet!" I screamed as I was going in. But I was wasting my breath. Decker was getting whipped around like a flag in a Lethbridge chinook.

My job in situations like this is to get close to the bull on the side opposite the cowboy and get hold of the rope to untie the guy. With a lot of the bulls, it's possible, but with one like this, you're wasting your time.

Still, they pay me to do something so I knew I had to go in. I'd never get hold of the rope, let alone stick around long enough to do anything constructive. My only hope was that the bull would fling the rider free before one of us got hurt.

And that's almost the way it happened. Ty Decker was flung free, and I had the satisfaction of seeing the cowboy scramble safely back to the chutes the instant before the bull got me. Again. With a couple of notable differences this time around. The first was that I was facing Richter Scale, which meant my backside was about the only part of my body that didn't get hurt. The second was that he fired me, not at Tub Willoughby's barrel, but at the chutes, specifically chute gate number five.

Chutes are made of sturdy steel pipe to ensure that bucking horses and bulls can't get out before they're supposed to. I can now testify that they're equally effective at keeping low-flying people from getting in.

That was the last thought I had for quite a while.

I regained consciousness in the ambulance in time to see my dad bending over me, his face a portrait of concern.

"I told you not to fight bulls on a Tuesday," he nodded knowingly.

"Today's Wednesday," I whispered.

"Sure it is, but if you hadn't tempted fate on Tuesday, this wouldn't have happened one day later."

The face of Rhonda Rae Crockett materialized, smiling as always, over my father's left shoulder.

"Don't worry about your dad, Doc. I'll take care of him until you get out," Rhonda Rae winked.

"Shit," I said and slipped into a black swirling fog.

Three days later I woke up to see the same two faces, except Rhonda Rae was no longer smiling and the grin on my father's face was slightly wider than the wingspan of a 747.

Dad was holding a newspaper. Rhonda Rae was holding Dad. I rang for a nurse.

"They did an article about me!" Dad said rather loudly.

Tubes were running from several openings in my body, my tongue felt like the top quarter inch or so had been filed off, and somebody was jackhammering his way out of my head through my right temple.

"How you feeling, Doc?" Rhonda Rae looked paler than usual, and she had bags the size and color of hockey pucks under her eyes. It occurred to the still-functioning part of my brain that Rhonda Rae might not have had much sleep.

I tried to answer her, but my lips were stuck together, and the effort it took to get them unstuck resulted in big-time pain in my left side.

"You have three broken ribs," Rhonda Rae said.

"You wanna hear it?" asked my dad.

"And a hairline skull fracture," Rhonda Rae said.

"There's a picture and everything." Dad held the paper about a baby-finger's length away from my face.

The nurse, a husky stern-faced woman with short cropped hair, came into the room and looked around the newspaper at me. I gestured with my arm, hoping she would understand that I wanted my dad removed from my presence.

She didn't. Instead, she said to Rhonda Rae, "Now that Mr. Allen has regained consciousness, I'm sure he'd like some time alone with his father."

As the nurse smilingly guided Rhonda Rae to the door, I invoked an old Armenian curse, which I couldn't remember exactly, but it had something to do with one's skin being removed while still alive, followed by immersion in flowing lava, capped off by an encounter with badly undernourished piranha fish. Anyway, that nurse was in deep shit; I had made sure of that.

Dad perched himself on the side of my bed and spent a couple of industrious minutes finding a comfortable position for himself, each movement he made sending a hot harpoon of pain through my side.

"I been boffin' Rhonda Rae," Dad said after he had finally fidgeted himself into a comfy pose. "I think I surprised her. I'm pretty sure she thought my refractory period would be a lot longer. But I been boffin' her steady ever since you got hurt."

This was the first "facts of life" talk my father and I had ever had. I wanted to say something about his brave show of concern for my well-being, but he must've read my mind and beat me to it.

"Don't think for a minute that I haven't been worried about you." Dad lowered his eyes reverently. "Damn worried. Rhonda Rae's just a stress release."

"I understand," I managed to get my mouth to say.

"Bet you never had 'er, eh?"

"Everybody's had Rhonda Rae, Dad."

"Not like me, boy, not like me."

I closed my eyes and let my head fall to one side, hoping he'd think I'd lapsed into unconsciousness again. Or died.

"Don't gimme that fake crap." He stretched the newspaper out in front of him. "I want you to hear this."

I opened one eye to watch him.

"I'll just give you some of the better quotes," he said. "How's this? 'I never met a bareback rider who didn't have hemorrhoids or a steer wrestler who didn't deserve to.'"

"You didn't really say that," I squeaked.

"Hell, that's nothin'. Listen to this one. 'There's three things that make this life worth living: riding great buckin' horses, makin' love to good women and runnin' over gophers as you're driving down the highway.'"

Dad jumped off the bed, bouncing the mattress as he did so, and I wondered if I'd ever been cursed by an angry Armenian.

"He wanted to do one of those articles about the concerned parent of a rodeo clown, but I think I gave him a better story. Don't you?"

"Way better."

The nurse came in then and told my father it was time to let the patient rest. I thought about telling her that I'd never rest as long as I knew this person was inflicting himself on Cloverdale and Rhonda Rae, but knew I didn't have the strength to say that many words. They left with Dad calling yet another quote over his shoulder, something about today's cowboys being mushmuffins compared to the hands of his day.

For a couple of minutes, I lay staring at the ceiling thinking about a theory an amateur actress I'd met once told me. She believed we chose our own parents, some weird cosmic thing that happened just at the moment sperm and egg united. If she was right, I had a lot to second-guess myself for.

The door opened and Rhonda Rae tiptoed in, looking over her shoulder. She crossed to the bed, bent down and kissed me on the cheek. She smelled good.

"I just came back to let you know that he's okay," she whispered. "I'm taking care of him."

"Rhonda Rae, if he has a heart attack while you two are having at it, I'll hunt you down and kill you with a poison blow dart." I took hold of her wrist, but my grip had the torque equivalent of light yogurt.

Rhonda Rae giggled. "What are you . . . did he tell you that we're . . ."

"He told me." I tried to sound disgusted.

"Doc, your father is a gentleman." She patted my hand. "He hasn't tried anything. Nothing. He's not like you."

She didn't need to throw in that last part.

"He's kept me up until the wee hours with his stories, but that's it." She giggled again. "He's been sleeping on the couch in my motel room. But, God, he loves to talk."

"Sorry," I mumbled.

"That's okay. I think it's kind of cute that he wants his son to think he's getting laid."

"Cute" is not the word I'd have chosen to describe my dad. Rhonda Rae winked at me and started to leave but then stopped at the door.

"By the way," she said as she turned to me again. "The only other thing he's been doing is coming to the hospital and sitting out there waiting for you to regain consciousness."

She was gone then, and I was left wondering if I should update my opinion of the amateur actress's theory.

Waking up to my dad peering down at me was becoming a habit.

The next time it happened, he was waving what looked like a couple of bookmarks back and forth in front of my nose. But I knew, given Dad's attitude toward reading, that they weren't bookmarks.

"Hi, Dad."

"Two tickets, forty-five yard line, to the Stampeders' first exhibition game," he grinned. "What do you think about that?"

To be honest, at that exact moment I didn't think anything about it at all. I was thinking about orange juice and how I'd cheerfully swap several of my vital organs for a glass of freshly squeezed.

"Great, Dad. We can go together." I tried to smile.

"Nope," he shook his head. "Sorry son, I can't go. I'm gonna be fishing about that time."

"I thought you didn't like fishing."

"Changed my mind. You remember the Claysmores? Phil and Doris? Nice folks. Well, they were telling me about a cabin they have at some lake or other. Apparently, there's fish in there plentiful as taxes, so one thing leads to another and I get myself an invite. Turns out Mrs. Claysmore has a younger sister . . ."

"Dad . . ."

". . . fiftyish or thereabouts but horny as hell and . . ."

"Dad . . ."

". . . so I figger what the hell . . ."

"DAD!"

"WHAT?"

"Why did you lie about you and Rhonda Rae?"

"What?"

"She told me you never laid a hand on her." I touched his arm. "You don't have to tell me that stuff about women to impress me. I'd be just as impressed knowing the truth, that you're not wild and crazy but just a hell of a nice guy."

"She lied."

"No, she didn't."

"How do you know?"

"Women don't lie about stuff like that. Men do."

"Yeah, well . . . maybe . . . but I could've. Had to practically fight the woman off. Didn't want to take advantage of a young girl like that."

"Yeah, right."

"If I'd known she was a blabber, I'd 've gone ahead and given her the ol' boom-boom. I mean, shit, I've got a reputation to maintain."

"I can understand your concern."

"Yeah, well you better not be blabbin', too."

"Your secret is safe with me."

"Good . . . good."

"And thanks, Dad."

"Thanks for what?"

"For . . . for the tickets."

"Enjoy the goddamn game," Dad said, and without looking at me, he pushed open the hospital room door and was gone.

CHAPTER FOUR

That explains how several weeks later, at a pivotal moment in my life, I was sitting in the thirty-second row on the thirty yard line of McMahon Stadium's west grandstand. Next to me was my longtime friend—well, what the hell, my only friend—Doug Carruthers. At about the eight-minute mark of the third quarter, I fell in love with the Calgary Stampeders' team mascot whose name was Ralph the Dog.

The Eskimos were second and seven on the Stampeders' forty-nine yard line when I realized I wanted to spend the rest of my life in a caring sharing relationship with Ralph. The Stampeders were trailing the loathsome Eskimos 31 – 3, which, given the talent of these particular Stampeders, was a flattering score for the homeside.

The only thing that surpassed my love for the pitifully inept warriors in red and white was my hatred for the Eskimos. I'd had the misfortune to live in Edmonton for several years and found Edmontonians to be, well, immodest. Insufferable is maybe a better word. I mean, this is a city that erects signs about itself at all the major roads into the city, signs that say City of Champions.

The best thing I can say about Edmonton is that it reminds me of Ottawa, where I spent two very long years of my life taking journalism and drugs—not necessarily in that order—at Carleton University.

When I was a kid in the fifties, the Eskimos were winning Grey Cups almost annually, due largely to a man named Jackie Parker, who had the speed of a barrel racer's horse and the moves of a barrel racer.

He could pass, punt and catch. He could also kick last-second field goals, which rested on the crossbar before falling inevitably on the Stampeders' side of the end zone like an east Calgary wino toppling from a curb. Parker was a leader of men, a student of the game, an inspiration. In short, he was probably the greatest football player ever to play in Canada. I hated him.

 Ralph was on the sidelines directly in front of us. He was holding up a cut-out letter D, which he would show to the stands on the other side, the idea being that the fans over there were to yell "De." Then he would hold up a miniature picket fence in our direction, and we would yell "fense." You get the picture—"De–fense, De–fense."

Except that Ralph wasn't getting much of a response, possibly because the Eskimos had scored damn near every time they got their hands on the ball. The fans were yelling things at the Calgary players, all right, but "De–fense" wasn't one of them.

When Ralph thrust the picket fence in our direction, there was virtual silence, except for a guy in a lumber jacket a couple of rows up from us who suggested that Ralph should stick the fence up Horner's ass, Horner being a defensive back who'd been beaten for three touchdowns so far.

I jumped up and yelled, "I love you, Ralph," as loud as I've ever yelled anything in my life and sat back down.

Some fans turned to look at me in the way that people have of looking at football-game drunks.

Doug also turned and said, "Why did you do that?"

"I love her," I said.

"Her? That's stupid," Doug said.

"There's a twenty-seven-year-old single mom in that costume, and I want to spend my life with her."

"How do you know that?" Doug signaled to a kid going by with a hot dog tray.

"How do I know a lot of the stuff I know? I don't know. I just know."

"Makes sense." Doug paid the kid and bit into his hot dog.

The Eskimos completed a twenty-four yard pass to Horner's man, and the guy two rows back yelled, "Hey, Horner, it ain't no coincidence that the first three letters of your name are the same as the first three letters of 'horseshit'!"

"They usually have pimply faced high school kids in those costumes," Doug said.

"I know, but this one's a twenty-seven-year-old single mom, and I'm nuts about her." I looked down and saw Ralph coming up the aisle, our aisle. He/she never did that.

As Ralph came closer, the lumberjack yelled, "Attaboy Ralph, you really got 'em up for this one."

Ralph stopped right beside me.

"I love you," I said.

"I heard you the first time."

"I know you're a twenty-seven-year-old single mom, and if this was a perfect world, we'd go back to your place after the game, throw some coals on the barbecue, listen to a few Irving Berlin tunes, make love while the coals are warming up and then have a couple of steaks and a bottle of red wine, quite dry," I said, looking into Ralph's large sad eyes.

"First of all, this isn't a perfect world, and second, you're an idiot," the voice inside Ralph answered.

"Sounds like a pimply faced kid to me," Doug said.

"Why did you come up here, Ralph?" I asked.

"Because I wanted to see what kind of dork would yell 'I love you, Ralph' at a football game."

"I'm a rodeo clown."

"I could have guessed half of that."

"I love the way you sort of flip your tail back and forth when the Stampeders get a first down."

"Blow it out your ass." Ralph started back down the aisle.

"Ralph is nothing if not cordial," Doug said as he downed the last of his hot dog.

Never ones to abandon a sinking ship—actually, this vessel had deep-sixed itself by the middle of the second quarter—Doug and I stayed to the end of the game. It ended 45 – 11 for the Eskimos. We were there for the last play, a thirty-six yard pass completion by the Eskimos over the inept backup who'd replaced Horner at the start of the last quarter. One thing the Stampeders had was depth.

It wasn't so much loyalty to the squad that kept us there as the need to finish Doug's mickey of V.O.

Even Ralph had disappeared to wherever team mascots go in the late stages of a massacre. I kept craning my neck, but she/he was gone. I spent the last few minutes of the slaughter looking at my bank book to see if I could afford a season ticket. I figured there'd be quite a few available.

Traffic in the parking lot was already thinning out by the time we got there. Doug, in an altered state of consciousness by then, was jumping back and forth in front of exiting cars yelling "De–fense."

When we got to Doug's car, she was there, leaning on a Thunderbird parked next to us. I knew her even without the paws and floppy ears.

"It's her," I told Doug.

She was wearing a leather skirt that did a lot more for her legs than the Ralph costume. It was warm enough that she was carrying her sweater, which meant her arms were bare. They were very nice arms.

"How did you know?" she asked me without moving from the fender of the Thunderbird.

"What?" I said.

"About me doing Ralph tonight. How did you know? My sister told you, didn't she?"

"You have a sister?" This was the first real interest Doug had shown.

"She's the only one who knew I was filling in for my neighbor's son."

"Your neighbor's son? . . ."

"Pimply faced kid? About fifteen . . . sixteen?" Doug asked.

"Goes to Crescent Heights High School," she answered.

"Bingo," Doug said to me. "This psychic shit is easy."

He wandered off to hassle a bus load of Edmonton fans, and I leaned on the bumper of Doug's car opposite the woman I adored. It was dark in that part of the parking lot so I couldn't see her as well as I wanted to.

"Seriously, how did you know?" she asked me again.

"You're going to think this is crazy, but I'm sort of psychic."

"In a pig's ass," the woman I love said. I can't say I wholly approved of her word choice. I wondered if she'd ever met Stan Shofner.

"I mean it," I said. "I've never met you or your sister before in my life. I just had this . . . feeling . . . something told me that there was a woman in the Ralph costume. Not just a woman but the woman for me."

"You really are an idiot." She sort of smiled when she said it.

"What's your name?" I asked.

"You're the one with ESP. You tell me," she said.

"I don't do names," I explained.

"I thought you said you were a psychic." She cocked her head to one side and looked at me.

"I am, but I don't do names."

"What do you do?" she wanted to know.

"Well, I'm one for one in the category of women in dog suits," I said.

"It's Angela, and you better rescue your friend."

I turned just in time to see Doug launch into a not bad rendition of our high school fight song from the hood of a Hyundai.

"He's all right." I turned back to Angela. "Look, if the steaks thing is out of the question for tonight, maybe you could just give me your phone number. I could call you, and we could plan our wedding or something."

"There's a problem with that."

"With what? The phone number or the wedding?"

"Both," she said as Doug returned. "I have a boyfriend."

That possibility hadn't occurred to me.

"Dump him."

"No."

"But we're cosmically right," I said as I took hold of one of her hands.

She pulled away. "Why do you talk like you're on drugs?"

"It's a practiced skill," I said. "Listen Angela, I don't care who your boyfriend is . . . . By the way, has it occurred to you that you came right to our car? You don't think there's something significant in that?"

"This is my boyfriend's car," she said, pointing to the Thunderbird.

"Your boyfriend was at the game?" I asked.

"He's one of the players." She nodded in the direction of the still-floodlit stadium.

"One of the Stampeders?" Doug asked.

"Yes."

Doug turned to me. "Only a desperate groupie would have anything to do with anyone on this team."

"Which one?" I asked. I figured I might as well know the enemy. I hoped it wasn't a lineman. Even an inept lineman can be bigger than a round bale, and some are downright mean.

"Dennis Horner."

I didn't say anything.

"Have you noticed that the first three letters of his name are the same as the first three letters in 'horseshit'?" Doug quoted the guy in the lumber jacket.

"He didn't have a good game," Angela said a little defensively.

"Now there's an under-fucking-statement," Doug said.

"Are you really a rodeo clown?" Angela asked.

"Yes, I am."

"Have you been to the Calgary Stampede?"

"Not in the last three years," I told her. "But before that, I was there for ten years in a row."

"How come you don't go there now?"

"I don't know," I shrugged. "They stopped hiring me. Maybe they don't think I'm good anymore."

"Don't the bulls scare you?"

"To death. Look, I know this all sounds like a bad pickup line, but it's the best I can do, so why don't you just give me your phone number? Your boyfriend is bound to be cut from the team in the next few days. Maybe then we could get together."

We were interrupted by the arrival of a very unhappy looking guy. It had to be Horner. He looked considerably bigger in the parking lot than he had from row thirty-two.

"What's goin' on, Angela?" Horner asked in the tone of a man who'd been beaten for three touchdowns.

"Nothing," she said. "These guys are just leaving."

I took out a pen. "So Angela, maybe you could just jot your phone number here on the cover of my program."

"I think it's time you two clowns hauled ass outta here." Horner took a threatening step toward us.

"I'll be damned . . . he's psychic, too," Doug said, hitting me on the arm. "Nobody even mentioned the clown thing, and here's ol' Dennis, making the connection. By the way, Dennis, has anybody ever pointed out that the first three letters of your last name are the—"

Doug's comment was cut short by what I thought was a pretty good right cross. It was the hardest hit Horner had made all night. Doug folded up on the pavement at Angela's feet.

Then it was my turn. I backed up as Horner began a charge at me that I suspected came right out of the "Fundamentals of Playing Defensive Back" handbook. I never played football, and I'm the worst fighter in the hemisphere, but I do have considerable experience getting out of the way of things that put their heads down to charge at me.

Actually, dodging Horner was considerably easier than evading a lot of the bulls I've had to contend with over the years, perhaps because—and I don't want to be unfair to Horner here—the bulls may have been smarter.

In any event, Horner hit the side of Doug's Marquis with enough force to effect about a six-hundred-dollar body shop repair bill and to knock himself senseless.

"You take yours home, and I'll take mine home," I said to Angela as I lifted Doug into the passenger side of his car.

I propped him forward to ensure that he did his bleeding on the floor mats, closed the door and turned to help Angela with Horner. The boyfriend was already sitting up, and I concluded that helping Angela was both unnecessary and injudicious in that it could result in my being killed if Horner were to suddenly complete his recovery.

"Goodbye, Angela," I said, scooping my program and pen off the pavement. "I love you. I have to go now, but don't worry. I'll find you, and we'll eventually live happily ever after with several fine strong babies."

I was crashing at Doug's apartment at the time, so after a couple of very quiet beers at the Highlander, we went back to his place.

The phone was ringing as we walked in the door. I answered it since Doug was still having trouble enunciating.

It was my ex-wife.

"I've been phoning all night long," she said.

"I was out," I told her.

"I guessed that." She took a deep breath.

"Everything okay?" I asked. "Nothing wrong with Larry?" Larry is our thirteen-year-old. I see him at Christmas and during school vacations, which isn't enough, and I was hoping Diane wasn't calling to say he wouldn't be coming this summer. But that wasn't it.

"No," she said. There was a long pause. "Dave, listen, I'm getting married."

There was another long pause.

"That's going to play hell with our reconciliation, Diane." I had the biggest craving for a cigarette I'd had in the four years since I'd quit.

"There was never going to be any reconciliation, Dave. You know that."

I gestured at Doug to toss me a cigarette.

"Actually, Diane, it's probably best this way." I lit the cigarette. "I'm getting married, too."

Still more silence. "Really?" Diane's voice sounded more irritated than surprised. "I didn't know you were seeing anybody. I mean I knew you were boffing buckle bunnies at a world-record clip, but I had no . . . Well, congratulations."

"Same to you," I said. "When's the big day?"

"We're not sure. We might just have a quiet ceremony at my parents' place." Diane's parents live in a nifty hacienda, about half a million worth in the hills near Salmon Arm.

"Great!" I was feeling a little light-headed from the cigarette. "Angela's parents are in Puerto Rico. She wants a big church wedding in San Juan. But I don't know."

"You lying bastard," my former wife said. "When are you going to grow up?"

"Soon, Diane, soon . . . . No shit. I can see more and more signs all the time. Pubic hair, my voice is changing . . ."

"Goodbye, Dave."

"Bye, Diane. The congratulations were sincere."

"Thanks."

I hung up the phone and sat down to finish the cigarette.

"Feel like talking?" Doug asked.

"Not with you," I said. "You mumble."

"You feeling fucked up or what?" Doug twisted a cap off a beer bottle and passed it to me.

"I hate it when you do Freud," I told him. "Besides, why would I feel fucked up? I'm forty-one years old. I've got enough rodeo contracts to keep me from starving for at least sixty days. The best woman I ever knew just phoned to say she's getting out of my life permanently. I'm in love with a lady who wears a dog costume. And the Stampeders are horseshit. I'd say things are pretty damn good."

"Well, when you put it like that . . . By the way, nice going. I didn't think you'd pull it off."

"What?"

"The phone number thing with Angela."

"Now you're not only mumbling," I said, taking a long drink of the beer, "you're also babbling."

"You mean you didn't see this?"

"See what?"

Doug held up the football program. There on the cover, next to a lipstick-drawn happy face, were the seven sweetest numbers I had ever seen.

At twenty minutes after six the next morning, I phoned Angela.

"Hello?" Her voice was soft and full of sleep.

"Does giving me your phone number mean that you've considered my marriage proposal in a positive light?"

"What?"

"I love you," I told her.

"Have you ever considered the more mundane elements in a relationship, like dating, for instance?"

"You think I'm pushy?"

"I don't even know your name."

"It's Dave. Most people call me Doc. How about breakfast?"

"No."

"Why not? I thought you wanted to date."

"No, I don't want to date. I just wondered if you'd thought of it. Besides, Dennis is coming over."

"He's not there now? You mean you don't live together?"

"No. Does that surprise you?"

"Yep. We're in the latter stages of the twentieth century after all."

"Well, we don't live together. Call me old-fashioned. Are you a doctor?"

"What?"

"You said they call you Doc."

"Oh, that. No, it turns out that I'm the reincarnation of Doc Holliday. You know, the outlaw from the Old West? A lot of people think I'm a little strange when I tell them that."

"Jesus, I can't think why."

"How about lunch?"

"I don't think so."

"Dennis?"

"No, it's just that I don't think I want to juggle two relationships at the same time."

"I can understand that," I said. "Lose Dennis."

"You're right."

"About losing Dennis?"

"About being pushy."

"Oh." I tried to sound contrite.

"What time is it?" Angela asked.

"Six twenty-five."

"Christ."

She wasn't happy. "Maybe we could do breakfast in two sittings," I suggested. "Me until seven forty-five, then Dennis until nine. I can bring my own dishes. They're very nice. What do you say?"

"I don't know if giving you my phone number was a good idea."

"It was a great idea," I said, "and as a gesture of good faith, I'm going to hang up now with a promise not to call you for at least, let's say six hours."

"Swell."

"We're going to be terrific together."

"You're weird."

"I knew I shouldn't have told you about the Doc Holliday thing."

"No, that's not it. You're just weird. Bye."

"Bye." I hung up the phone, pulled on my jeans and a T-shirt, and walked a couple of blocks to a Chinese café. I drank a cup of coffee and read the *Sun.* I skipped over the Sunshine girl, a habit of mine since I dated a feminist who told me there's a direct link between guys ogling the Sunshine girls' body parts and the violence against women we read about in the rest of the paper every day. That made sense to me so I stopped ogling.

The headlines looked uninteresting so I flipped directly to the sports pages. My mood picked up in a big way when I read the story on the game. The football writer called Dennis Horner a red-and-white water buffalo and, later in the story, a zit on the face of the Stampeders' defense. I figured Horner had twenty-four hours, tops.

I went back to Doug's apartment. He was up and getting ready for work. He had some kind of accounting job for a trailer company. He wasn't real talkative, but if my eyes and mouth looked like his, I wouldn't have been saying much either.

"Do you think I'm crazy?" I asked.

"Is this a trick question?" He was still mumbling a little but not as bad as the previous night.

"I'm serious," I said. "Do you think I'm nuts to fall in love with a girl in a dog costume? Maybe I'm just reacting to Diane getting married or something."

"You fell in love with the dog, if you'll pardon the expression, before you knew Diane was getting married. And to tell you the truth, given a lot of the things you've done in your life, this would fall into the category of normal behavior."

"Good points, both of them," I concurred. "Want to grab some eggs on your way to the office?"

I thought he was going to throw up.

"Raincheck."

"What are you going to tell people at work?" I pointed to his lips.

"I'll tell them I was hit by a missed field goal," he answered. "What have you got on for today?"

"Well, I thought I'd flip through *Heart of Darkness.* I'm in the mood for black symbolism. Then I might phone Angela thirty or forty times."

"You don't think you'll turn her off?"

"Can't see it. She's nuts about me."

"Right." Doug smacked his forehead with his palm. "See ya. Oh, by the way. Somebody from a rodeo in Grimshaw phoned yesterday. They want you to work it."

"Terrific," I said. "Everybody who's anybody, and a few people who aren't, go to the Calgary Stampede, but I get to go to someplace called Grimshaw."

"The number's by the phone."

"By the way, hold your weekends open. Angela and I'll be marrying soon, and I'm holding out for you as best man, although Angela mentioned Dennis Horner as a possible."

"Should be a hell of a wedding." Doug stopped at the door to look at me. "She'll be in her Ralph costume, the dogcatcher can give her away and you can wear your clown outfit. I wouldn't miss it."

As he was closing the door, I yelled, "On second thought, I don't think we'll invite you."

Doug had given me an idea. I phoned Angela's number.

She sounded more awake but not any happier to hear from me.

After we got the hellos out of the way, she said, "I thought you said you wouldn't phone. You break your promises."

"What I have to say takes precedence over promises. I'm going to a rodeo tomorrow. In Medicine Hat."

"Don't call me collect."

I chose to ignore that. "But that's not why I'm phoning."

"Uh-huh."

"I have to go to Grimshaw in a couple of weeks."

"Why am I getting confused?"

"For a different rodeo. That's what I do, remember?"

"Of course. I must not have been concentrating. So give me your fascinating travel itinerary again."

I decided to ignore her sarcastic tone, too. "Medicine Hat tomorrow, Grimshaw in two weeks," I said.

"I don't know why I'm asking this question, it's certainly not because I give a damn, but where the hell is Grimshaw?"

"It's a beautiful spot. I think we should honeymoon there."

"I have to go. Somebody's at the door."

"If it's Dennis, tell him goodbye for me. He'll be gone soon. Don't forget, I see things."

Angela hung up.

The next morning I was off to Medicine Hat, and on the stillest hottest afternoon I can remember, I tried to keep bulls from maiming cowboys half my age. It was my first time back since I'd been hurt at Cloverdale. Since no barrel man had been hired, I was also expected to crack wise for the rodeo faithful. I wasn't particularly effective on either count.

When the performance was over, I went to the stock contractor and told him I was leaving. The stock contractor, Rex Keller, was huge, and although he was a much better guy than Stan Shofner, I wasn't tickled with the way he looked at me.

To my surprise though, Rex shook my hand and wished me luck. He and I were the only people in the world who knew I had just clowned my last rodeo. I'd known it was time for quite a while but hadn't admitted it until that moment. The decision probably had a lot to do with Angela. My obsession with rodeo had already cost me one good woman, and even though my chances with Angela were less than outstanding, I was determined that rodeo wouldn't be the deciding factor this time.

Rex and I swapped a few courtesies. "It's a big man who knows when it's time to move on," and crap like that. A half hour later I caught a ride back to Calgary with a couple of steer wrestlers.

Dad showed up at Doug's place about twenty minutes after I got back. That surprised me because he knew I was supposed to be in Medicine Hat for four days. It occurred to me that maybe psychic ability was inherited.

What surprised me more was the guy he was with. Suits and my dad tend to avoid each other, even when the suits are on other people.

"You forget I had a rodeo this weekend?" I asked.

"Shit, yeah, I did. It's this goddamn aging business. So, what are you doin' here? You get another horn up the ass?"

"Came home for a beer," I told him. "Come on in."

They did and I got more beer while they sat on what passes for a couch in Doug's place. Its problem is that Doug likes it for romantic interludes with the various women who drift in and out of his life and apartment. And because Doug is pretty much a traditionalist in the sack, he sticks to the missionary position, which has created a well-developed sag in the couch.

When I came back with the beer, Dad and the guy in the suit were sitting pretty close to each other, the sag acting as a kind of buttocks magnet.

"You quit, didn't you?" accused my dad as I handed him and the suit a beer.

"Yeah." I sat in the chair that went with the couch. It didn't have a sag. That's because, to my knowledge, the only kinky thing to have ever taken place on it happened at a party we'd thrown the Christmas before. An aerobics instructor with a bosom that stretched damn near to Montana decided to do a naked demonstration of jumping jacks in time to Rod Stewart's "Do You Think I'm Sexy?"

It was a big moment at the party, and the great thing about it was she didn't destroy the chair. Actually, she fell off during Rod's second chorus and broke her left ankle, which resulted in some hastily contrived explanations for the ambulance attendants.

"I figured you were fixin' to quit," Dad said. "This is Vince Jeffrey."

The guy didn't look like a Vince. A Mark maybe, or a Stephen, but not Vince. I figure a Vince has to be minimum six-one, maybe a hundred and ninety pounds, big shoulders and a nose that can't hold up glasses because it's been flattened in some long ago pugilistic encounter. This Vince was five-ten, tops, with sloping shoulders and a little girl's nose.

He looked uncomfortable, but that may have been because he and Dad were tilted toward each other so that their heads almost touched.

"Pleasure to meet you," he said.

"Hi," I waved.

"It's Tuesday," Dad said. "It figures you'd abandon your livelihood on a Tuesday."

"It's time I retired," I told him. "Besides, you don't want me to fight bulls on Tuesdays. This way I won't, ever again."

"Vince here is a movie producer. He saw the article about me in the paper, and he wants to make a TV documentary about my life. It's bull-shit to quit in the middle of a rodeo."

I looked at Vince. He was obviously having trouble following Dad's method of conversing, which was . . . well, directionless.

"Mm-mmm," I said in an attempt to be noncommittal.

Vince was trying hard to achieve the perpendicular on the couch. He wasn't succeeding.

"It's a kind of docu-drama," he said. "We'll tell the story of rodeo, the history, the color, the texture, as seen through the eyes of a rodeo clown, your father's. We think it'll be wonderful."

He pronounced it as "ONE-derful," which I guessed was the artistic pronunciation.

"The texture?" I asked.

"Yes, you know, the subtleties, the fabric, the weave of the sport."

He made it sound like a tie.

"Of course," I nodded. I'd been rodeoing for a quarter of a century and had no idea the sport had texture. Or any other characteristics one normally associates with haberdashery.

I wasn't really in the mood for Vince, and I think Dad sensed that. He tried getting up but succeeded only in bumping heads with his guest. Both of them tried to act like it hadn't happened. Finally, they got up together, and after getting their bodies back in plumb, they looked at me and then each other.

"This may not be a good time," Dad told Vince. "He's pretty ugly tonight. I can tell."

"But surely he'll come around when we tell him about his part in the film," Vince said in a stage whisper.

I took a long drink of the beer, then got up and went to the kitchen. I figured if they were going to discuss me in the third person, I'd go make myself a grilled cheese.

The frying pan was warming up, and I was slicing cheese when they came into the kitchen.

"It's a pretty good offer," Dad said.

"How good?" I asked without turning around. "You want a sandwich?"

"No thanks," Vince said. "We anticipate the shoot taking two to three weeks. And I expect that you and your father would be paid about fifteen to twenty thousand each. Those would be minimums, of course."

"Of course," I swallowed.

"Can I get a toasted bacon, lettuce and tomato?" Dad asked.

"No problem, except we've got no bacon, no lettuce and no tomato. Which leaves you with toast. Still want one?"

"Pass."

"So what do I do in this movie?" I asked.

"Well, Mr. Allen . . ."

"People call him Doc," Dad interrupted.

"Well . . . Doc, we just want you to be you. And, of course, you'll stand in for your father in the dangerous parts."

"Dangerous parts?"

"Well . . . the scenes with the bulls."

"You want me to fight bulls?"

Dad hiccuped. "What the hell else do you think they'd want you to do . . . act?"

"I'm retired."

"Oh." Vince sounded subdued. I liked him better that way.

"Listen, you dumb-ass punk," Dad suddenly yelled at my back. "You've fought bulls most of your adult life, in places called Bald Knob, Arkansas, a lot of the time for a couple of hundred bucks a day. Now you finally get a chance to make some real money, and you're standin' there with your back to us, frying a goddamn sandwich and treatin' this man like shit. What the hell is your problem?"

I flipped the sandwich over and turned to look at Dad. He was perceptive. There was a problem.

"It's a woman," I said.

Dad walked around the kitchen table and looked me the way people look at their shoes when their feet hurt.

I'm not sure what Vince made of it all, but he wrinkled up his little-girl nose. Then Dad broke into a wide grin. When he grinned, all the lines on his face were emphasized and he actually looked his age. I hadn't noticed that before.

"Shit, is that all?" he laughed and winked at Vince. "I thought maybe it was something to worry about. Women are nothing to worry about. Besides, they're all crazy about movie stars."

I didn't think Angela would be crazy about a movie star. However, she might find a guy with money more appealing than someone with an overdraft, lots of bills and no job.

"Maybe I'll phone her," I suggested. "See what she thinks."

"Good idea," Dad nodded.

Vince just shrugged.

The movie moguls followed me back into the living room, and I dialed Angela's number. It rang for a long time, and she was out of breath when she answered.

"Hello."

"Hi, it's me."

"Oh," she said. "I thought you were going to be away. Doing what rodeo clowns do."

"I was but I'm in intensive care at Foothills Hospital. I got stomped and they're operating in a few minutes to take out my spleen, my liver, my pancreas and both kidneys."

"Oh, my God, that's . . . Wait a minute . . . . Is this another one of your bullshit deals?"

"Yeah, it is, but you were concerned for a second, admit it. Good to see that, Angela. It's a positive sign. Truth is, I've had a change of plans."

"Uh-huh."

"Uh . . . look . . . I was wondering. I've been offered some work in a movie. I'm interested to hear how you might feel about that."

"What makes you think I'd feel anything at all about it . . . or you for that matter."

"Just some crazy idea I had, I guess."

"Well, you're wrong. Well, not totally. You're right about the crazy idea part. I have zero interest in your life."

This was harsher than necessary, and I sensed some trouble, romantically speaking. "You know, Angela, you've got this playing-hard-to-get thing down to a science. You can quit any time."

"Who's playing?"

"There's danger in the movie. I could get hurt. For real this time."

"Uh-huh."

"I won't do it if you don't want me to. I mean if you're going to worry and fret."

"I think I can handle it."

"I see. So you want me to do it then."

"Listen Dave . . . Doc . . . Dave . . . Dammit, I wish you didn't have two names. I don't give a damn if you do the movie or not. Are you following me on this?"

"Uh . . . yeah . . . thanks. Well . . . bye then."

I hung up and looked at Dad and Vince.

"She's totally in favor," I said.

Vince reached out, took my hand and shook it for a long time. When he finally let go, I went back to the kitchen to look at my sandwich. It was charred on one side.

"Uh . . . Mr. Allen," said Vince, who, along with my dad, had followed me to the kitchen again. "I've already mentioned to your father that things could move quickly on this so I'll probably be in touch in the next few days. Is that all right?"

"I've always heard that movies take forever to get off the ground."

"Not if the money's in place. You'll be hearing from me very soon. You'll be around for a while?"

"I'm not going anywhere." I took a jar of strawberry jam out of the fridge and began to apply jam liberally to the top of the sandwich.

Vince made a face, and I heard Dad explaining as they made their way toward the door. "He's always done things like that. But he's a good kid, really. He'll be wonderful in the movie."

He pronounced it "ONE-derful." I bit into the sandwich like I wanted to hurt it.

Vince Jeffrey wasn't kidding. Things moved very quickly. Three weeks after the meeting in Doug's apartment, Dad and I were sitting in a plush motor home at the rodeo grounds in High River, a town about three quarters of an hour south of Calgary. Vince was across the table from us.

We were there to sign our contracts, and filming was to start that afternoon. Dad's pay was going to be twenty-two thousand smacks and I'd receive sixteen-five. My hand kept creeping toward the pen. I wanted to sign fast.

Then I wanted to phone Angela. I'd phoned her exactly two hundred and seventy-one times in that three week period and hadn't reached her once.

Dad was in no hurry to sign anything. He was wearing sunglasses and a Hawaiian-looking shirt. I think he figured that's what movie stars wear. I'm pretty sure he was doing Jack Nicholson. If that's what he was doing, he wasn't that bad.

"So, Vince," Dad pulled a cigarette out of his shirt pocket, which I knew was part of the act because he hadn't smoked in about twenty-eight years. "Whaddaya say we have a look at the script?"

"Sure," Vince was grinning. At least his face was. The rest of him you could tell was tense. "I've got it right here. But I should tell you, we've only scripted the first part of the show. We want to leave it open-ended so we can build in a lot of your own recollections and anecdotes as we go."

"Light?" Dad stuck the cigarette in his mouth.

"Actually, I'd prefer that you didn't smoke in the motor home." The grin had faded, and Vince was beginning to look unhappy.

"We've got a little problem here," Dad said as he thumbed through the few pages of script Vince had set in front of him.

"What's that, Mr. Allen?"

"Call me Hoot." Dad reached in another pocket, pulled out a lighter and lit the cigarette.

Vince reached back and slid open one of the windows in the motor home.

"See, I'm a little worried about authenticity." Dad waved the cigarette around. Not much of the smoke was going out the opened window.

"Authenticity?" Vince puffed out his chest. It wasn't much of a chest, but what there was was puffed out. "I don't think you need to worry. We have a fine scriptwriter. A talented woman from Vancouver. She won an award last year for a screenplay about a member of Greenpeace."

"Greenpeace." Dad said the word with the same inflection people use when they say "diarrhea."

"And of course, you'll both have a lot of input into the script," Vince said. His chest was de-puffing, and I thought I noticed a few drops of sweat on his forehead. It was hard to tell for sure through the smoke cloud my father was producing.

"Exactly," Dad nodded. "But I wonder if maybe we should formalize that input."

"Formalize it?"

"Yeah." Dad butted the cigarette. "Now I'm not questioning the talent of the Greenpeace lady, but I'd feel more comfortable if we had someone working with her with a little more background in this particular subject area."

Vince didn't say anything, but he was opening and closing his hands a lot.

"I have someone in mind who I think would be a real asset to the project," Dad said.

"I don't think so, Mr. Allen . . . Hoot." Vince put on an assertive face.

Dad looked out the window of the motor home at the activity going on in the arena. "Lot of stuff," he said slowly. "Cameras, crew, technicians—must be expensive as hell."

Vince knew what was coming and didn't bother to look out the window.

"We had a verbal agreement." He sounded whiny. "I thought cowboys were supposed to be honorable people."

"Two things." Dad looked back at Vince. "First of all, we aren't honorable at all. We've had a couple hundred years of having to fight like hell for everything we get in life, whether it's food, women, recognition or money. Cowboys have gone nose to nose with floods, fires, stampedes, rustlers, crooked landowners, storms, bullets, snakes and, in our case, bulls. There's not a lot of room for honor there."

It was quite a speech. Dad must've stolen it from some rodeo publication or a Louis L'Amour novel. He wouldn't have read the whole book of course, and I wasn't sure why he was going on like this, except that my father enjoys pissing people off. And Vince Jeffrey was the kind of guy almost anybody would want to piss off.

"The second thing is we verbally agreed to be in the film. And we talked price. We never discussed script or writers or any of that." Dad let his voice soften a little. "I'm only thinking of the success of our project."

He put a lot of emphasis on "our." Vince moved around some, and the vinyl on the motor home seat made a considerable amount of noise.

"You have someone in mind?" he looked unhappily at Dad.

"Yep," Dad grinned. "The perfect partner for the West Coast broad."

"Who is it?"

"Him." Dad moved his head in my direction.

Ever since I first figured out that somebody was actually in charge of creating the words that go on pages, I've wanted to be one of those people. Thing is, I've told damn few people about that. And my father was not one of them.

Vince and I inhaled in unison. He spoke first.

"I'm sure that—"

"He's a writer." Dad cut him off. "I've seen the stories and stuff he's written. He's got 'em hidden, but I've seem 'em. And they're damn good. And he knows this sport better than anybody I can think of."

"I'm sure that's true, but . . ." Vince looked at me like my dog had just crapped on his carpet. "Uh . . . maybe we could use you as a script consultant."

I'm pretty sure Dad was lying about reading all the stuff I'd written, and even if he had, he wouldn't know good from garbage. Still, he'd done a hell of a job on Vince. I was almost convinced myself. Even so, I was about to do the self-deprecating bit—Oh, gee, Dad, I don't think we should bother the nice man—in the way Canadians are taught, but something stopped me. Maybe it was the hatred, tinged with disgust, on Vince's face, or maybe it was the realization that when it came to literary agents, I could do a lot worse than Hoot Allen.

"You can call him anything you want," Dad went on, "but I want his name on the credits under "Screenplay" . . . and, of course, the Greenpeace chick's name can go there, too. In fact, it can even go above his."

"Well, uh . . ."

"And an extra ten thousand in his contract."

"That's ridiculous."

Dad gazed out the window again and fumbled around like he was looking for another cigarette. "Jesus, will you look at that? Another truckload of equipment arriving."

"Five thousand," Vince said without moving his lips.

"Seventy-five hundred."

"Sixty-five."

"Where do we sign?" Dad held out his hand like Vince Jeffrey was his oldest friend. For a second I thought Vince was going to stamp his feet or cry or do whatever guys like him do when they're angry.

I was grinning so hard, my jaw muscles were threatening to seize up. I was a writer! Better than that, a writer with income!

Mordecai, W.O., Farley, Doc—damn, I liked the sound of that.

CHAPTER FIVE

That night, after the first day of shooting, which mostly consisted of standing around looking at camera angles in the rodeo arena, I went back to Doug's apartment and made call number two hundred and seventy-two.

Angela answered, "Hello?"

"Geez, I've missed you," I said.

"I was away."

"Oh."

"I went to Vancouver to visit my parents."

"That's great," I told her.

"How's the movie business?"

"Okay, I guess. We just started today."

There was a long silence on the line.

"Dennis was cut from the team last Friday." Angela's voice caught as she said it.

"You're kidding!" I yelled into the phone. "I must have missed it in the paper."

She was quiet again. I realized I hadn't reacted as sympathetically as I might have. "It's . . . uh . . . hard to believe." I couldn't bring myself to say "that's too bad."

"You predicted he'd be gone a long time ago," Angela reminded me testily.

"Well, yeah, but it wasn't one of my psychic predictions. It was just, you know, a prediction. I figured they couldn't keep anybody that bad around for very long."

I heard a sniffle at the other end and knew I still wasn't saying the right things.

"I mean, to his credit, he lasted about fifteen days longer than I expected," I added quickly. "Which is good, you know . . . I mean if . . . you know, you're looking for a positive note in all of this."

"Have you ever considered getting a job on one of those distress lines?" She was being sarcastic but hadn't hung up, which was a good sign.

I waited a few seconds, sort of like a mourning period. "So, is he gone yet?"

"Shit," Angela said. I wasn't sure if she was referring to me or the situation in general.

"Look, Angela, I didn't even know the guy'd been cut, honest. Although, I will say my cosmic center has been radiating the way it does when something good's about to happen. I know how you must feel, but maybe this is for the best, don't you . . . ?"

"It's too soon to be having this conversation. I can't talk about it yet." She sounded like she was crying.

"You're right, of course," I said and forced myself not to add anything smart ass, though a thousand possibilities came to mind.

"I know you're going to find this hard to understand, but I cared a lot about Dennis. I miss him."

"Miss him?" I repeated. "You mean he's left town . . . as in forever . . . history . . . toast . . . swallowed the olive . . . a bad memory?"

"You creep."

"I'm sorry, Angela, I really am. As a matter of fact, I really do know exactly how you feel. I found out the other day my ex is remarrying, and it shook me up bad. I think my behavior was probably pretty childish when she told me."

"Gee, that's not like you."

"I deserved that," I said. "Anyway, I apologize and from now on I'm going to make a real effort to be more sensitive."

"Well," I heard her sniff, "all right. I'd appreciate that much consideration."

"Right. Now about the wedding. Do you want one attendant or two?" She hung up.

I called her back. "Don't hang up," I said as fast as I could. "I swear to God, I'll be a perfect gentleman. Please, Angela."

"Do you know your little witticisms can get real boring real fast?"

"I do know that. It's just my way of covering up my insecurity, which doesn't excuse it, I realize, but so help me I'm going to be serious for the next two minutes, and then you can hang up."

"Two minutes and then I'm gone . . . toast . . . history and all the rest of that shit."

"Will you have dinner with me?"

"Maybe. In a year or so."

"I was thinking of tonight."

"Why would a relatively sane, well-adjusted woman want to have dinner with you?"

"I don't know." I had to be honest with her. "But, listen, they're bringing bulls onto the set tomorrow. It's not out of the question that the horn of some three-quarter-ton Big Mac on the hoof could ventilate my body. How would you feel if you refused a dying man his last request?"

"Is this one of your psychic premonitions?" She sounded a little too optimistic for my liking.

"No, actually it's not. Truth is, I've looked ahead, and it turns out that I'm going to live to be one hundred and six, and you and I are going to have seven or eight—"

"Don't start with me. By the way, you've got fifteen seconds."

"Dinner."

"Okay."

"Okay?"

"Yes."

"Yeah!" I high-fived Doug's toaster off a shelf, and it crashed into a lot of pieces.

"It's that big a deal to you?" Angela's voice sounded a little softer.

"Yeah," I said, "it really is."

Angela wouldn't give me her address so we agreed to meet at Miccio's, a terrific Italian place where they serve real Italian food and talk real Italian. To each other. To me they speak broken English, but the great thing is I did them a favor once, I can't remember, got some cowboy's autograph or something. Anyway, whenever I go there, Mama Miccio and the gang treat me like I'm some kind of hero.

And the even greater thing is, Angela suggested the place. Damn, life's beautiful.

I had to hustle to get there on time because Doug's car was still in the body shop, and he had the GMC, which left me to take a bus. I had to transfer twice, but I was right on time. Angela was already sitting at a back table in a black dress that could have been from a Fred Astaire-Ginger Rogers movie. She looked gorgeous, and sexy . . . but not sexy . . . all at the same time. You know what I mean? She was sipping a glass of red wine.

"You look sensational."

"What's that?" She pointed to the package I was carrying under my arm.

"A toaster."

"You don't like the food here?"

"It's for Doug. I was in such a great mood I thought I'd get him a present."

"And you bought him a toaster?"

"Yeah, I'm kind of a sentimental guy."

"You must have been a big hit with your wife on anniversaries."

"I always bought her lingerie. She never wore it. She had a drawer in her dresser with seven hundred dollars worth of kinky sleepers, and she never wore one goddamn outfit."

"Are you going to sit down?"

I hadn't realized I was still standing. "Yes."

Mama Miccio came out of the kitchen. "Doc!" From her mouth the name sounded like a bottle of rum-based liqueur.

"Hi, Mama."

She stopped suddenly when she got to our table and looked at Angela.

"Angelina." Mama Miccio touched a weathered hand to Angela's cheek.

"Angelina?" I said.

"Doc," Mama said, turning and leaning toward me, "I no like the girls you bring here before. But this . . . now this is a girl."

"My feelings exactly, Mama."

"What are you going to have, my children?" She leaned into Angela. "He's a good boy, Angelina."

"So he keeps telling me."

"Why don't you surprise us with something wonderful, Mama?" I suggested.

"Ah, for you I make tonight the magic, okay?"

"Okay, Mama."

"Angelina?" I said again after Mama had left.

"Dennis and I came here a lot."

For a minute I was angry that she had suggested we come to "their" restaurant. "I notice Mama didn't mention him. Didn't say he's a good boy. Did you notice that?"

"Taste the wine," she said as a waiter brought a bottle that made me wish I'd been less impulsive about letting Mama order for us.

For years I've worked out the cost of things on the basis of how many bulls I have to face to pay for it. In a three-day rodeo, there's likely to be sixty bull riders entered. I get paid about six hundred dollars per rodeo or ten dollars a bull. Mama had decided on a five-bull bottle of Italian red.

The first hour of the evening went very well. Angela told me she liked baseball better than football, and I told her I liked baseball better than rodeo. We had other things in common, too. Like our embarrassment at living in a province with Don Getty as premier, a shared hostility for zucchini and root canals, and an appreciation bordering on ecstasy for Miccio's escargots in garlic butter.

She told me about her work in the registrar's office at the university and about her daughter Patti, aged nine. I didn't mention my work but did tell her about Larry and my GMC, aged twenty-nine.

I surprised Angela by telling her I didn't like country music, and she surprised me by telling me she did. We were halfway through the magic Mama Miccio "for us tonight had made" with veal and canneloni, when I decided I'd try something I wasn't used to with women—honesty.

Angela asked if I'd like to do anything else besides rodeo. I've been asked that question before, and I usually go for witty: Well, actually I've considered several things—lion taming, performing hormone implants in the breasts of beautiful but small women and my real, as yet unfulfilled, desire, the circumnavigation of the globe in a float-equipped '55 Plymouth. It's stupid, I know, but it avoids having to engage in real conversation. This time I wanted to have a real conversation.

So I said, "I've always wanted to write."

Angela blinked and said, "Really?"

"Yeah, I've done a little. Had a couple of short stories published in some pretty small magazines and a few poems here and there."

"Is this for real?"

"Yeah, I'm serious." I felt embarrassed as I said it, which is probably why I didn't make a habit of telling people about that side of me. "I'm actually going to be doing some of the script for the film."

"I think that's great," she said.

"You do?" I figured if she was going to like me at all, it would be because of the macho cowboy thing. That's what usually pushes buttons with the women who hang around rodeos. But here was someone who actually seemed impressed because I wrote. I guess I was used to Doug who always intimated that the written word was considerably less important to the survival of mankind than, say, the NHL draft.

"Can I see something you've written?"

"Are you kidding? You actually want to read some of my stuff?"

"Yes, I do." She looked at me as she said it, and I knew at that moment I could cheerfully murder Dennis Horner if he tried to come between me and this woman.

"Okay." I reached into my pocket and took out a piece of paper, writers being a lot like new fathers with baby pictures. We always have our latest creations with us, ready to inflict them on unsuspecting victims. "I've been working on this for the last couple of days. It was inspired by a picture of an Indian encampment I saw on a postcard in a drugstore."

I handed it to her and she read it.

Then she read it aloud, her voice doing things with the words that made me think for the briefest of seconds that maybe I could really write.

As I look beyond my village at the red hills rising high,
Overhead I see the eagle flying free in cloudless sky.
And often in the morning all alone I question why.
Standing at the water's edge, I watch and watch and sigh
But the river gives no answer; it just rolls on . . . rolls on.

Then the woman calls out to me; on her face I see a smile,
And I smell the sweet meat cooking, and hear laughing from our
     child.
Still the question keeps returning in the gentle and the wild
As I walk the water's spongy bank for mile on twisting mile,
But the river will not answer; it just rolls on . . . rolls on.

In the middle of the village, in the middle of the day,

I seek a moment's quiet and to Great God I do pray,
Always mindful of the question, but the answer stays away;
Then I look back to the water. Has it nothing more to say?
And the river shrugs and ambles, rolling, rolling on.

Will I ever find my answer? Will I ever know this truth?
Will I know more as an elder than I do now in my youth?
Are we only to accept this world, this life, this joy, this song,
Leave the river to its silence on its journey swift and long
And never more to ponder thoughts so difficult, so strong,
Content to share the bond of time, one day, one dusk, one dawn?

She looked at the paper for a while longer, then at me. "I thought 'with it' poetry wasn't supposed to rhyme."

"Shakespeare's rhymed," I said, "and he was fairly with it."

"It's old-fashioned."

"It's about an old subject."

"Maybe a little trite."

"I can tell you're crazy about it."

"It's sexist."

"How so?"

"'The woman.' I hate that—'the woman.'" She jabbed at the page.

"I thought 'woman' was today's politically correct designation."

"But you don't say 'woman.' You say 'the woman.'"

"But it isn't said in a derogatory or condescending sense. If it had been a man he saw, he would have said 'the man,'" I explained.

"No, he calls their child 'our child,' but he calls his wife 'the woman.'"

"You're right," I agreed, "and in our society I can see that might have a kind of sexist connotation, but in that society I don't think that was the case."

She looked at the poem again. "Maybe," she nodded. "Anyway, I like it." She handed it back to me.

"I thought it was trite, old-fashioned and sexist."

"It shows a side of you I would never have guessed existed. I thought you'd write stuff about Cowboy Bob and the killer bronco, Widowmaker. This is reflective. It's almost pastoral."

"Yeah, well it's really a diversion between chapters of the Cowboy Bob story. I'm at the part where Cowboy Bob's dog, Spike, has just saved the life of Rosie the Rodeo Queen. You see there was a runaway pickup truck and Rosie—"

"I do like your poem," Angela smiled, and my forty-one-year-old heart did a little flip, something I thought I'd outgrown with puberty.

"Keep it." I pressed it back into her hand. "I'd like you to have it."

I was having a tough time keeping myself from trying to push events ahead at a faster than natural speed. I mean, dinner was going very well, but it's a quantum leap from pasta, even great pasta, to a lifelong relationship with someone. And halfway through our first date, I was more positive than ever that this was the woman I wanted to spend my life with.

As the waiter topped up our wine glasses, Angela said, "About Grimshaw."

"Oh, all right, you can come. Now will you quit begging?"

"You really are funny sometimes," she laughed, then added, "but not all the time."

"I understand."

She looked at her wine glass. "I can't come to Grimshaw."

"Let me guess. You have to wash your hair."

"No, that's not it."

"It doesn't matter. I'm not going to work the rodeo. I've retired. Of course, I think you and I should go anyway."

Angela didn't say anything for a couple of minutes. She took a sip of wine, reaffirming a conclusion I had come to earlier that this was a woman with ONE-derful lips.

"I'm going to Dayton," she said.

"Datin'? As in playing the field?" I honestly misunderstood. "Angela, I'm not kidding. You won't find anyone anywhere better for you than—"

"Dayton, Ohio," she said. "Dave . . ."

"Call me Doc. People only use Dave when they're going to say something bad."

"Doc, just before I left to come to dinner, Dennis phoned."

"Maybe you better call me Dave."

"He wants me to come down to his place for a while, to see if we can make it together."

"In Dayton fucking Ohio?" I said it much too loudly, and several unhappy faces turned in our direction.

"Are we going to be able to discuss this like adults?" Angela was also unhappy.

"I'm not sure. I doubt it. In the first place, what does Dennis do in Dayton that you'd like to be a part of?"

"Well, he's not a rodeo clown, that's for damn sure."

I didn't have an answer for that.

"I'm sorry. That was uncalled for, and mean." She put her hand on my arm. "He'll be going into the family business. Some kind of insurance."

"It figures." I pulled my arm away. "I might have known there'd be old family money in there as part of the attraction."

"Now you're being unfair. Money doesn't have anything to do with any of this. I don't love you. That's the issue here."

I took her hand and put it back on my arm. "Angela, listen to me. I know this is all happening really quickly."

I was looking at her hand as I talked and trying to imagine holding it twenty-five years from now. Unfortunately, my psychic powers weren't in the mood right then. "But if you do go down there, then that's it. You'll never know if we could be good together. Why don't you at least keep your options open?"

"How does staying here with you keep my options open?"

"It doesn't," I said, grinning at her. "I just like the sound of it a lot better. Listen . . . Dennis and Angela . . ." I said it in a sort of ditz voice and she laughed.

"Okay, now listen . . . Angela and Doc." I tried to sound like Lorne Greene. "Has a nice ring to it, doesn't it?"

She laughed again.

"And something else, I've been to Grimshaw and to Dayton." I lied. "Dayton has black flies the size of pigeons, the garbage collectors have been on strike for eight years and gangs of rampaging Cleveland Indians fans roam the state, taking the lives of innocent Canadians whom they suspect of being Toronto Blue Jays supporters.

"Grimshaw, on the other hand, is a virtual paradise of bubbling streams, cool evening breezes and sensational Italian restaurants. In fact, while the rodeo is in town, there's also a rock concert with The Rolling Stones and Bruce Springsteen together for the first time—"

"I don't like rock, remember?" Angela gently raised her eyebrows.

"Right, did I say Bruce Springsteen? I meant Garth Brooks, and not only that—"

"Doc?"

"Yes?"

"Would you like to make love?"

"Jesus, talk about changing the subject," I said.

We looked at each other for a long time.

"Here? Now?" I looked around. "These people were upset when I said 'fucking.'"

She didn't answer but kept looking at me. There were little smile wrinkles in the corners of her eyes.

"Actually, Angela, I have to say no." I had to fight to keep my hands from going for my throat. "The truth is, there aren't many things in this world I'd rather do than make love with you. But there is one. And that's to be with you, for the long haul." It sounded like a cliché as I was saying it, but I couldn't think of anything better, the words not having been invented to express what I felt at that moment. "I have a feeling this is probably a way of saying goodbye, and although it'd be the greatest goodbye this cowboy'll ever know, it's still goodbye. And goodbye isn't where we should be with this. So I guess it's thanks but no thanks."

It had been a long time since I'd been with a woman, that myth about cowboys and a never-ending parade of gorgeous sun-bronzed women being just that, myth. Either that or it doesn't apply to rodeo clowns. And it had been a couple of lifetimes since I'd been with anybody like Angela, so I was making a major sacrifice and not one that all parts of my body seemed to agree with.

The bill came; perfect timing. "Can I at least buy you dinner?" she asked. I noticed she still had her hand on mine.

"Yep." I tried to grin. "I'm not that goddamn chivalrous."

For a while we didn't say much. I was wishing like hell I could think of something that might change her mind. And I knew I wasn't going to come up with anything.

"When are you leaving?" I asked her finally.

"I don't know . . . in a few weeks I guess. There are some things I have to do first."

And that was it. The evening was over. I stood up, picked up the toaster and started toward the door, Seventeenth Avenue and the bus back to Doug's place.

"Oh, Doc," Angela said, stopping me as I headed for the door. "By the way, your psychic powers must be slipping a little."

I turned back to her. "How's that?"

"I'm actually twenty-nine," she said.

"That isn't the only thing I was wrong about." I thought it was a terrific exit line, but it didn't bring Angela diving at my ankles to keep me from walking out of her life.

The evening wasn't a complete loss. A Mary Steenburgen flick was at one of those closet-sized mall theatres in north Calgary. It was *Time After Time,* a not bad movie in which Mary is pursued by Jack the Ripper, who's been transported to modern day San Francisco in H.G. Wells's time machine. Sounds ridiculous, I know, and I'd seen it before, but I thought it'd keep my mind off Angela for a while. It didn't. But it did keep me from trying to forget lost love in the more traditional manner of consuming life-threatening amounts of Seagram's products. Which I suppose was good.

And Doug liked the hell out of his new toaster.

CHAPTER SIX

When I got back to the apartment, I wasn't tired so I stayed up, made a bowl of popcorn and read over the completed part of the script. I was surprised to discover that it was very good. The only changes I made were to cross out the words "cowpoke" and "buckaroo," which the Vancouver writer had made considerable use of. I didn't bother to substitute other words for the ones I crossed out.

Working on the script didn't interest me a lot, but at that moment, neither did life. Especially my life. Especially my life without Angela. Pretending to work had merely been a ploy to divert my attention from the fact that for the second time in my life, a fabulous woman wanted nothing more to do with me. The ploy wasn't working, and I still wasn't tired, so I took to drawing little buckaroos and cowpokes with huge genitalia all over the margins of the script. Childish, I know, but more diverting than the pretense of work.

Doug arrived home about four, dead drunk and in the company of a redhead who said "like" about every third word and drank gin right out of the bottle. She was Doug's kind of girl.

"So like I go, 'Like, what do you want me to do? I've got a life of my own, you know. What do you, like, want from me, for Chrissake?'"

I gathered she was relating some long ago conversation to Doug, who was incapable by that time of comprehending. They stopped when they saw me sitting in the chair in the living room. Actually, the redhead stopped, and Doug sort of slid into her.

She took a drink of gin. "You didn't tell me you had, like, a room-mate. He's cute. Hi."

"Like, hi," I said.

"I don't have a roommate," Doug slurred. "I've never seen this fuck-ing guy before."

It occurred to me that comprehension might not be the only thing Doug was incapable of at that moment.

"Geez, I could, like, phone Ellie, and we could get us a party going, eh?"

I tried to picture what a friend of this person's could possibly be like and even imagined a dialogue between the two of them. Scary.

"Sounds great," I said, "but I can't. I'm in therapy right now. I'm try-ing to deal with an overwhelming sexual desire for members of the Canadian Senate, either sex. Until I've resolved this, my doctor, Doctor Cramden, Doctor Ralph Cramden—you may have heard of him?—says I should avoid involvement in relationships with anyone outside the Upper House."

Doug slid down onto the couch and all but disappeared in the sag.

"Oh," said the redhead.

I was fairly certain that that was as in-depth as our conversation was likely to get so I excused myself. I took the script to bed with me, rea-soning that spending the rest of the night with people who said "yippee" and "yahoo" would be far better than taking part in what was going to happen in the living room.

The next morning when I went downstairs, Doug's friend was asleep, fully clothed, on the couch, her legs draped over one end and her head resting at a ninety degree angle in the sag. She was snoring.

Doug was nowhere to be seen, which led me to believe that at the last minute he had come to his senses and run off into the night to escape a fate worse than death, as they like to call it in the old westerns. Whoever said that even when sex is bad, it's pretty good never met the person Doug had brought home the previous night. I crept into the kitchen and deposited a couple of Eggo waffles in the natty new toaster. Tradition says that the owner should be first to use a new appliance, but I was hungry and didn't give much thought to tradition.

Doug appeared in the kitchen as I poured myself a glass of juice. I looked at him, then handed him the juice. It's impossible to describe his skin color without using terms familiar to those in the mortuary business. As bad as he looked, however, he smelled worse. As I crossed to the cupboard for another glass, I was careful not to touch him, which would have meant condemning the clothes I was wearing to immediate cremation.

"Where did you sleep?" I assumed the relationship hadn't been consummated.

Doug downed six ounces of Tang in a swallow. "I dunno. In the basement, I think."

"We don't have a basement," I reminded him.

"Really?"

"There's a girl in the living room." I wasn't sure he'd remember.

"Nice?" he asked.

"I was going to ask you. Red hair."

"Oh, yeah . . . Rita."

"More juice?"

"More juice."

For the second time, I gave him the glass I had planned to drink, then, figuring we could do this for a long time, swigged some for myself right out of the jug.

"She said something about you two being engaged," I said cheerily.

"That's not funny. What day is this?"

"Wednesday."

"Do I work Wednesdays?"

"Usually."

"Damn."

"I don't recommend you work this Wednesday, unless you want to get fired. You better phone in sick."

The waffles popped up. Doug looked at them. "I can do sick," he said. "Maybe I'll go grab a shower."

I poured syrup on the waffles as he headed for the bathroom.

"If Rita wakes up . . ." he said.

As if on cue, the noise from Rita's sinus cavity increased by a decibel or two.

"Yeah?" I said.

"Don't tell her about me." Doug stumbled off in the direction of the shower without explaining what it was about him I wasn't supposed to tell Rita. The question was academic because when I'd finished the waffles and was on my way out the door, script in hand, the chainsaw concerto was still issuing from the sag in the couch.

The day on the set began with a dispute about where the cameras were to be located during my first bull-fighting sequence. Vince wanted a couple of guys with handheld cameras in the arena with me. I explained to him that this particular strategy would likely result in the bull rider, me or the two guys with the cameras, and maybe all four of us getting killed.

Vince seemed less troubled by this prospect than I had hoped, but he finally relented when one of the technicians explained that the cameras were probably worth more than the entire budget for the film.

A cowboy named Bucky Nichols—honest, that was his name—was the stunt man who would ride the bull, a big bruiser from a small-time amateur contractor in the area. The bull's name was Crash Course. He had a fair set of antlers. In honor of my co-scriptwriter, I suggested loudly that we change Bucky's last name to Roo, but nobody got the joke. Maybe they hadn't read the script yet.

Dad wasn't required for the scene and was not on the set, which upset me more than I liked to admit. I figured he could have been there for the first dangerous part of the thing, especially since it was him I was standing in for. And he could've handled the arguing with Vince, which would have left me free to get ready for the scene. As I was entering the arena from under the announcer's stand, Vince stopped me. He wanted me to meet Jacqueline Lang, the scriptwriter.

She surprised me, first of all by looking a lot better than I thought she would, and then by telling me she was looking forward to working with me. She looked like she meant it. She was forty-fivish, I guessed, with a terrific smile and a figure that looked like it had been looked after. She also gave you the feeling that in a set-to with Dad or anybody else, she might be a worthy opponent. I shook her hand and headed into the arena, which was now clear of handheld cameras.

Bucky wasn't one of the bull-riding legends, and it took him about ten minutes to get ready. There isn't that much to do. You put on your chaps and glove, the bullrope is passed around the girth of the bull and you "warm it up." This consists of rubbing resin into the rope to make it sticky. Then you set your hand into a kind of handhold, take the tail of the rope into the hand as well, slide up so you're virtually on top of the rope—and your hand—and nod your head. The gate opens and the interesting part begins.

The better and more courageous bull riders perform all the preparatory tasks quickly and get on with the ride in a minute or two. This, of course, can be complicated by a bad bull, one that won't stand still in the chute. Crash Course wasn't one of those. He stood quietly, paying almost no attention to Bucky's endless chatter and clumsiness.

I got a little fed up after a while. "Are you going to ride that bull or make love to it?"

"He's not that easy to get out on," Bucky whined.

"He hasn't moved a goddamn muscle. Get on and nod your face," I snapped.

At last he slid forward, twitched around for another few seconds and finally nodded.

The gate opened. The bull came out and circled slowly to the left, not showing much power or speed. I didn't figure it would look all that good on camera, but I did what I could to salvage the shot. I worked right at the bull's head with one hand on a horn. He followed me a little, but not a lot was happening. After a few seconds, Bucky jumped off and I took the bull away from him, which wasn't hard because Crash Course seemed largely uninterested in the proceedings. Bucky was excited as hell, and gave me a high five and a grin like he'd won the world title.

I walked back out of the arena and shrugged in the direction of Jacqueline and Vince. I figured they'd be pretty disappointed and want to do the bit again with a different bull.

But they were ecstatic.

"Wow!" Vince was beaming.

"That was really something," Jacqueline said. "How do you do that?"

I smiled modestly and kicked the dirt, cowboy style. I stopped short of saying "shucks." I was afraid it would end up in the script.

"I guess I'm just used to it."

My moment of glory was short lived. It was suddenly and noisily overshadowed by the arrival of my father. He was perched on the back of the biggest Harley Davidson I'd ever seen. Driving the motorcycle was the biggest person I'd ever seen.

The guy had a beard that stopped just north of his belly, which, by the way, extended a very long way past his belt. He was wearing sunglasses and a scarf tied around his forehead. He was everything I'd ever stereotyped a biker to be.

Dad jumped off the Harley, talking at the same time. I know this only because I could see his lips moving. It wasn't possible to hear anything over the sound of the bike, which wasn't as loud as the combined noise of a Guns 'n' Roses concert and an F-18, but pretty damn close. Finally, the large guy shut the thing off, and we picked up Dad midsentence.

". . . a ride over here this morning to see what we're up to." Dad stopped then and looked at us to gauge our reaction. But inasmuch as we had missed the real meat of the statement, which presumably dealt with details, like who the hell the motorcycle guy was, the reaction mostly consisted of open mouths and stunned faces.

Dad evidently figured this out and after a minute or so said, "I want you to meet my friend Suzy."

Suzy stood up then and stepped away from the bike. I used to do some cattle buying so I'm fairly proficient at estimating the weights of large animals. I pegged Suzy at real close to three hundred and fifty pounds. And even though a lot of his tonnage came in the form of fat, the sheer bulk of him, combined with the tattoos, leather and jewelry, made Suzy a very imposing figure.

"Suzy and his friends are having a little convention get together at a campground about three quarters of a mile from here," Dad explained. "He wanted to come over and say hi."

Suzy made a sound that resembled a bathroom noise more than "hi," but everyone appeared willing to give him the benefit of the doubt, and the sound, whatever it was, was greeted with a chorus of hi's, how ya doin's and yo, Suzy's. I looked over at Vince whose complexion had taken on the color of pissed-on snow.

"Actually," Dad went on, "that isn't Suzy's only reason for wanting to drop over this morning. He wants to challenge us to a ball game. Us against them."

I glanced around at the group and noticed that eye contact had dropped off to a minimum with Dad's announcement.

He was undeterred. "Tomorrow night, over at their diamond. Should be fun, eh?"

"We . . . uh . . . might . . . be shooting late tomorrow." Vince's voice sounded hopeful or maybe wishful.

"We can't go that late," Dad argued. "Come on. It'll bring us all together as a group, cast, crew, and who knows, maybe we'll kick some butt over there."

I looked at Suzy to see if he thought Dad's "kick some butt" line was funny. It was hard to tell through the facial hair, but I don't think he was amused.

"You bring the ball gloves; we'll bring the beer," Suzy said. "Game time is six-thirty." It wasn't a big speech, but considering that most of us hadn't thought him capable of verbalization, it was significant. And it appeared to settle, once and for all, the issue of whether or not there would be a ball game.

He climbed back on his bike, cranked up the engine and roared off down the road. And I don't use the term "roared" in a figurative sense. For the next couple of hours, the attitude on the set could best be described as subdued. I suspected a lot of us were mentally composing wills, last letters to loved ones and other pre-death correspondence.

At lunch, Dad met Jacqueline for the first time. I introduced them as we sat down to Chicken à la King from the catering truck.

"You're the Greenpeace . . . woman," Dad accused.

I was relieved he hadn't used "chick" or "broad" or "babe" in this, his first exchange with Jacqueline.

"I wrote a show about Greenpeace, yes," Jacqueline answered. "Pass the cream, please."

Dad passed the cream. "So that probably makes you one of them animal rights activists."

"I believe animals have rights, yes." Jacqueline smiled and looked at Dad in a way that suggested he drop the subject.

Dad leaned forward and his eyes narrowed to hard slits. "You're eating meat." He jabbed his fork in the direction of Jacqueline's plate.

"Yes, I eat chicken." She demonstrated by taking a mouthful and obviously enjoying it. "I also eat red meat, though in moderation, but that doesn't mean I think we should treat animals inhumanely."

That sounded reasonable as hell to me so I thought I'd try to lead us into new territory. "What other shows have you worked on Miss Lang, or is it Mrs. Lang?" I asked.

"Why not just Jacqueline? Well, let's see. I did a series on mountain climbing that was really interesting. We visited some of the world's tallest peaks. And then there was a one hour special in—"

"There's nothing inhumane about rodeo," Dad blurted.

"Dad, nobody said there was," I pointed out.

"You sound a little defensive," said Jacqueline.

"Defensive, my ass." Dad hit the table hard enough to rattle the cutlery five or six seats down. "I'm just tired of these Greenpeace geeks and the K.D. Lang's and the rest of the do-gooders trying to destroy our western heritage."

"Do you feel a need to call people who disagree with you names, Mr. Allen?"

I figured I'd make one last stab at lightening things up. "Why not? Our politicians do it all the time."

"True," Jacqueline nodded but kept looking at Dad. "For the record, Mr. Allen, I have done quite a bit of research on the subject and happen to believe that k.d. lang is at least partly correct. There are abuses in the beef producing industry, and as a matter of fact, I'm very concerned about calf roping in your sport, too. Though I have no scientific evidence to support the contention that roping calves around the neck and jerking them to a halt hurts them, I'm equally certain that you don't have scientific evidence that it doesn't. It certainly looks unpleasant."

"Oh, yeah?" Dad had stopped eating and was sort of snarling at Jacqueline, a sure sign that he was in trouble.

"Nice response, Dad."

"Shut up." To his credit, Dad was returning Jacqueline's stare. In fact, his eyes were no longer slits but large round orbs of shining rage. "Name one practice in the beef production industry that's even slightly inhumane."

"One?" Jacqueline responded. "How about three just off the top of my head. Hot-iron branding, sawing off horns with a wire and feeding cattle hot feed, namely barley, which destroys their livers."

"We have to identify our cattle, and we de-horn them for their own protection," Dad said.

"True, and I don't dispute the rationale for those practices. I merely question the methods used."

"And something else." Dad didn't give any indication that he had actually listened to what Jacqueline had said. "I've never in all my years in rodeo, and that's a bunch of 'em, seen a calf with a neck injury. A few broken legs, yes, but that can happen just as easy out on the range. But no neck injuries. They're not built the same as we are, you know." He'd switched gears, going now for condescension.

Jacqueline appeared to focus on the content rather than Dad's method of delivery. She laid down her fork. "Surely, Mr. Allen, you would agree that not all injuries are visible to the naked eye."

"Doesn't matter. The simple fact is—"

"Mr. Allen, I don't have statistics, and they're often meaningless anyway, but assuming you're correct and the calves aren't injured, can you feel good about an activity that gives the perception of being cruel?"

"She has a point there, Dad," I said.

Dad looked at me and shook his head sadly. "Wimp."

I shrugged and Jacqueline picked up her fork again. "Whether or not roping hurts the calves, it looks like it hurts them and that's why the event is unpopular at a lot of rodeos," she said quietly.

"Who says it's unpopular?" Dad challenged.

"You've seen it, Dad, and so have I," I interjected. "People leaving or looking away during the roping or cheering when a cowboy misses a calf."

"Bull twaddle."

I took a deep breath. I wasn't sure if continuing the discussion was worth the price I'd pay later in terms of whining and bitching. I decided it was.

"I was at a rodeo once," I looked at Jacqueline while telling the story, "and a little kid was standing against the arena fence peeking through the rails. A guy came out and roped and tied. The guy was fast, real fast, but suddenly, in one of those cemetery quiet moments that happens sometimes, the little kid yells, 'You let that baby calf go.' Tell you what, the kid got the biggest cheer of the afternoon. I felt sorry for old Dick Leatherbee, the announcer, trying to get the crowd back on track after that. I was standing with a couple of bull riders, not exactly the do-gooders of society, and one of them said, 'They're gonna have to do something about this shit or it'll kill it for all of us.'"

"So now I suppose you want to get rid of calf roping altogether because some whiny snot-nosed—"

"No, actually I don't," I said. "But I do think things can be done, rule changes and so on, that would make it less distasteful to people watching. And if we don't do something, then the real radicals of the animal rights movement in all their misinformed and uninformed glory are going to have a field day."

"But it's not cruel now."

"Maybe not, but that's not how it looks to the guy from Oakville seeing his first Calgary Stampede or the family from Sooke taking in an afternoon at Cloverdale. Or that little kid at the fence."

"But that's just the point." Dad waved an arm for emphasis. "The kid didn't understand, the same way the tree-huggers and animal lovers don't understand. This is part of our heritage. Calves have been roped on ranches for a century or better. It was the only way to doctor 'em and do the other things that were needed."

"That's true, Mr. Allen," Jacqueline nodded. "But my research indicates that the method of roping at rodeos is quite different. To make the event faster and more exciting it has become considerably harsher than what takes place on the ranch. Calves are jerked to a stop in order to save a few tenths of a second on a stopwatch. It needn't—"

"Your research, your research. Well, lady, your research sucks." Dad stood. "This is just great! Now we've got us a writer who's gonna paint the sport of rodeo so goddamn black—"

"Not at all, Mr. Allen," Jacqueline said. "In fact, I agree that rodeo is a rich part of the western experience. And I happen to personally love the excitement, but pointing out the flaws doesn't detract from the validity of the sport."

"Yeah, well we'll see. I'm going to round up ball gloves for the game. I hope like hell nobody's going to object because it's cruel to some critter that the glove used to be part of."

"Dad," I hated to have to disagree with him twice in a row, "I don't know if the ball game is a real good idea. I think a lot of people here might be a little uncomfortable with—"

"I might've known you'd chicken out." His eyes had become slits again.

"Actually," Jacqueline stood up, "I think a ball game might be fun. Maybe I can help you line up some ball gloves, Mr. Allen."

"Don't bother sucking up," Dad started off. "I can look after it myself."

"Mister Allen," Jacqueline's voice rose for the first time. "I do not suck up. If you don't think you can use a three fifty-six hitting second baseman on your team, fine. Go and get the gloves yourself."

Dad turned back and faced her. "Three fifty-six?" His eyebrows went up.

"Coquitlam mixed slow pitch league. Provincial champs two years in a row."

"This isn't slow pitch."

"I can hit a hard slider, too."

Dad shuffled from one foot to the other for what seemed like a long time. He appeared to be making up his mind about a lot more than who was going to play second base.

"Come on," he said finally.

Jacqueline smiled at me and went around the table to join my father, who did not smile at me. They walked off with the body language of a couple of grudgingly respectful prize fighters in the early rounds of a long bout.

Bucky Nichols stumbled up beside me. He had apparently done a lot of celebrating since his ride. "We . . . did some . . . great work out there today . . . eh, Doc?"

"I'd stay sober if I were you, Bucky," I said, knowing the advice was a little late. "I talked to Vince, and we're going to re-shoot your ride tomorrow. With a real bull this time."

I'd seen guys with a lot more talent than Bucky try to ride with hang-

overs. It usually turned out ugly. I left him in a state of advanced discomfort and wandered off to ponder whether I could hit a hard slider.

Weather conditions were, despite our prayers for monsoon rains,
perfect for the game. Our team was apparently not a big draw on the
road as only about twenty spectators were hanging around the periph-
ery of the ball diamond. These mostly consisted of huge-bosomed, T-
shirted girlfriends of the bikers.

I knew we were in trouble when our opponents showed up wearing
uniforms, this being an indicator of a certain level of seriousness and
maybe even proficiency. This was offset somewhat by the fact that most
of the players insisted on wearing their leather jackets over the tunics.
They called their team the Halos.

Jacqueline, a positive thinker in the extreme, suggested it was "kind
of neat" that our opposition had the same emblem as a major league
team from California. I explained to her that the name and the emblem
probably had more to do with the name of the gang, Satan's Halos.

Suzy was their pitcher. I watched him warm up. My misgiving over the
slider dissipated when I noticed that if Suzy had a breaking ball, he didn't
actually throw it, relying instead on the hard stuff. The distinguishing feature of Suzy's fastball was that once it left the pitcher's massive hand, no
one, least of all Suzy, had the vaguest notion of its final destination.

One point of concern for our team was that, as big as Suzy was, he
was of only average stature when compared to the rest of the bikers. I
was pretty sure our team wouldn't initiate any dugout clearing brawls.

Dad would be pitching for our squad, he alone claiming to have had
previous experience. He mumbled something about Little League. That
meant his last mound appearance had been approximately fifty-one
years before. What was notable about Dad's fastball was that he didn't
have one. In fact, what he threw, for the most part, could best be
described as a molasses ball, the strategy apparently being that if the
pitch took long enough getting to the plate, boredom might set in for
the batter and, with luck, he would nod off.

I had recruited Doug for the game. I was sure he at least knew which hand the glove went on, which placed him several notches above some members of our team. He would catch Dad's offerings, assuming any of them escaped the menacing bats of the Halos.

I was on first, which earned me the nickname "Who" with my teammates in a lone moment of jocularity leading up to the game. Morale seemed to be a problem with our squad, the result, no doubt, of the belief that the upcoming match was a threat to our survival. The Halos, on the other hand, were having a hell of a time. In particular, the three women on our team, including Jacqueline at second base, appeared to be causing considerable mirth among our all-male opposition.

Vince had agreed to be our manager but insisted on coaching from third base. This may have been because the Halos' dugout was along the first baseline. Vince refused to budge on this point, even when several of us suggested it was extremely unlikely we would ever get a runner to third base.

The bikers were surprisingly traditional, at least regarding baseball and its rituals. The game started with the playing of the national anthem on a stereo system rigged up to one of the Harleys. It was a solemn moment, and several of the Halos even left off smoking until very near the end of the anthem. This was followed by the customary managers' meeting at home plate. From where I was sitting, Vince didn't appear to be having much input in the meeting. When he got back to the dugout, I asked what he and Suzy had discussed.

"I'm not sure. He said 'fuck' a lot, and I thought it best to agree with him."

"Good strategy," I agreed. "By the way, where's the umpire?"

"Uh . . . that did come up . . . . There isn't one. Suzy and I agreed to use the honor system."

Doug overheard this part of the conversation. "Are you crazy? Nobody plays ball without an umpire. Especially against these guys."

"Okay, smartass," Vince placed his hands on his generous hips, "you go out there and tell them we don't think they're honorable men."

Doug thought about that. "Aw, what the hell, eh? Who needs an umpire anyway? Right?"

There was a murmur of agreement through our dugout, which, by the way, was a little crowded because it was also the storage area for the beer. I guessed from the number of cases the bikers had piled in there that they had anticipated a bigger turnout of fans, say five or six thousand.

We made a big mistake in the top of the first inning. We scored a run, the result of three hit batters and a sacrifice fly by Jacqueline. Doug, our lead-off hitter and first recipient of a Suzy heater in the ribs, was the runner on third and when he tagged up, I screamed at him to fall down or fake an injury or leave the base early, anything but score a run. I was concerned what the result might be if we pissed the Halos off.

Doug ignored my sage advice and scored standing up. While my teammates were high-fiving all over the place, I stayed in the dugout and studied the opposition. There were several unmistakable signs that we had pissed them off.

It quickly became evident in the bottom half of the inning that the infield was the best place to play. The first three Halos' batters all hit line drives over our outfielders' heads. One thing the Halos lacked, however, was team speed. So, as the clean-up hitter came to the plate, the bases were loaded. I wondered how far one of them would have to hit the ball to leg out a double. I didn't have to wait long to find out.

The clean-up hitter was Suzy. I could tell he was serious when he stepped into the batter's box because he carefully laid whatever it was he was smoking on the ground behind him. Suzy hit Dad's first pitch so hard and so far, everyone over forty on our team was unable to follow the flight of the ball. Our outfielders, who before the pitch had cleverly taken up positions a couple of townships from home plate, did not move as the ball went over them, still in the rise of its arc.

"I think you missed the bunt sign," I told Suzy as he puffed by me, but he didn't laugh.

I was certain the game would never get to the second inning, but miraculously we got out of the first on a pretty double play that Jacqueline started. We were only down eight to one.

The accident of the first inning did not repeat itself, and we did not score in our half of the second. The Halos added nine runs in the bottom of the inning. Suzy came to the plate twice. The first time was a repeat of his earlier appearance. The second time he managed only a triple as his stamina appeared to be wearing down. To give credit where it's due, containing Suzy's offense on this occasion may have been due partly to a piece of managerial brilliance on Vince's part. We employed something called the "Suzy shift," which meant only Dad and Doug were in the infield. The other seven members of our squad took up positions about a sixteen-dollar cab ride away.

Being held to a triple seemed to upset Suzy, and he decided to steal home on the next pitch. With Suzy's speed, the result was a long and stress-filled moment in Doug's life as he stood at home plate, ball in hand. Suzy was building momentum as he rumbled down the baseline. Suzy with momentum was a scary thing.

Doug, given ample time to think, devised what I felt was a pretty good strategy. He chose not to block the plate. Instead, he ran up the third baseline, circled around Suzy and tagged him on the backside as he headed for home. Suzy crossed the plate, his arms raised in triumph.

"Safe!" he roared.

This time Doug did not think. "What are you talkin' about you fat-ass dip-shit? I tagged you on that monstrosity you call a butt."

Suzy bent down, picked up his cigarette, placed it in his mouth and said, pretty quietly under the circumstances, "What did you say?"

I had taken off for home about the time Doug enunciated "fat-ass."

"He said 'safe,' Suzy, that's what he said." I pulled Doug toward the mound.

"Bullsh—" he started to say before I got a hand over his mouth.

"Are you trying to get us all killed?" I hissed when I got him to the mound.

"I tagged him for Christ sake." Doug pulled away from me.

"I know you did," I said, "but Suzy wants to be safe, and that's good enough for me. I don't really care if you want to commit suicide, but I'm sure they won't be satisfied with one lone skinny corpse, and I still have a few things to do in this life."

Doug humphed and grumbled but didn't say any more. The Halos got six more runs and left the field with a 21 – 1 lead.

"The honor system, terrific fucking idea!" Doug snarled at Vince as we headed into the dugout.

During the third inning, Doug decided that if the beer was going to be stored in our dugout, we should at least get to drink some of it. He cracked open a case, passed them around and was on his third himself when it was his turn to bat. I was on second base, having bunted my way to first and then advanced when Suzy walked Dad.

Doug set his beer bottle, nearly empty, on the exact same spot as Suzy had set his smoking materials during each of his at-bats.

"Try throwing strikes for a change, Slim," Doug challenged as he dug into the batter's box.

I wanted to cover my eyes but decided against it in the event that Suzy tried to pick me off second base. Not watching when Suzy threw a ball in your direction could result in extended unconsciousness.

Suzy, however, was not interested in me. "Where'd you get the beer?" he asked in a not entirely cordial way.

"Over there," Doug indicated the dugout. "Same place as I'm gonna get my next one and the one after that."

I'm pretty sure the Halos intended to share the beer with us after the game. However, it appeared Doug had, by helping himself, failed to observe some unwritten rule of biker baseball etiquette. Suzy didn't say anything, but his body language suggested that Doug was playing his last game. The first pitch was easily the hardest Suzy had thrown so far, and though I'm no radar gun, I had that baby clocked in the mid- to high eighties. It sailed past Doug in a line extending just behind his head and struck the backstop with enough force to push several fence links permanently out of shape.

"Strike one," snapped Suzy.

"Bullshit," replied Doug.

"Strike one!" Suzy took a couple of steps toward home.

"Pitch the goddamn ball." Doug took his practice cuts with a renewed sense of purpose. I had seen Doug drink before, God knows, and I was aware that for him, three bottles of beer were not even a start toward impairment, so I was at a loss as to what lay behind his death wish.

Suzy's next pitch would have sent Doug home in a body bag had he not ducked while Suzy was still in his windup. The pitch went by home plate at exactly the spot Doug's left cheekbone had been milliseconds before. I figured we better call the game, the only problem being that I wasn't sure how we could do it without incurring the wrath of the entire Satan's Halos' organization.

"Let me guess," Doug said as he straightened up. "Strike two."

"That's right, Peckerhead," Suzy said as he massaged the ball, presumably not to soften it up.

"Hey, Manager," Doug yelled at Vince, who was conducting a careful study of his shoes, "why don't you dispute the call? What are you doin' out there anyway?"

"I thought . . . I thought maybe it caught the corner," Vince shrugged.

Then Jacqueline stepped out on the top step of the dugout and called, "Okay, Doug baby, take this guy deep."

I thought her gesture heroic but a little futile. Here we were in a game that I would have been happy just to live through, and the Greenpeace lady was engaging in baseball chatter.

It got worse. Dad stepped off first base. "Attaboy, Doug buddy, you're the man now, baby. This guy's nothin'."

Next, a couple of the technicians got involved, and soon the entire dugout was a cacophony of meaningless baseball babble.

Even Vince, who wasn't exactly from the Billy Martin mold, hollered, "You can do it, Doug. Hit that old potato."

The shortstop for the Halos walked over to me and spit a substance the color of old mud onto the ground just in front of my shoe. He was wearing a hat band that said "Wink" on it. I wasn't sure if that was his name or a command. I took no chances and closed one eye, but I don't think he noticed. He pointed at home plate.

"That man's gonna die," he said matter-of-factly.

"No doubt about it," I nodded.

Doug stepped up again and took more practice swings. Suzy went into his windup, which mostly consisted of maneuvering his pitching arm so it wouldn't strike his extensive midriff during the delivery.

The pitch must have got away from him, or maybe the growing uproar from the visitors' dugout shook him up. Whatever the reason, he grooved the pitch. For the first time in the game, a Suzy offering was headed right down the middle of the plate. And Doug, in the words of Jacqueline, took the guy deep.

Well, not that deep. It was, however, a solid line drive to the gap in left center. The center and left fielders had either never seen that happen before or didn't want to risk some cardiac problem by actually going after the ball. Anyway, they didn't move. The ball rolled for a while and then came to a stop in the prairie wool that served as outfield grass. Doug dropped the bat, picked up his beer and drained it at home plate before he started down the first baseline in a jog-trot designed to irritate the opposing pitcher. When I crossed home plate, I glanced toward the mound. Suzy was watching Doug's every step around the bases. And his eyes were a color I'd never seen before.

In the outfield, neither of the Halos' fielders had begun to move for the ball. In fact, they were engaged in a rather heated argument about whose responsibility it was.

"Get the fuckin' ball," the left fielder grunted.

"You get the fuckin' ball," said the center fielder, "I got the last one."

"That was two years ago. Besides, I gotta bat in the next inning."

"We all gotta bat in the next inning. Maybe a couple times. Go get the goddamn ball."

Wink trotted out to short left field and said something none of the rest of us could hear. Wink, by the way, was the largest of the Halos, a fact that apparently was not lost on the outfielders. Amid much grumbling and kicking of outfield turf, the two disgruntled athletes moved slowly in the direction of the baseball. My attention was re-directed toward Suzy, who was now at home plate awaiting Doug's arrival. Had it been me, I'd have settled for a triple and the relative safety of third base. Doug, however, had no such intention. He rounded third and was hippety-hopping homeward.

Suzy had set his glove on the ground. This was not, I guessed, so that he could shake the hand of the homerun hitter. As Doug neared the plate, arms raised and a positively stupid grin on his face, Jacqueline and the rest of the team rushed out of the dugout. Jacqueline placed herself between Suzy and Doug, and offered the high five. Apparently, the Halos' honor system included a clause about not striking members of the opposite sex who played second base on the other team. Suzy hesitated and in that moment the rest of the team surrounded our hero and escorted him to the dugout. That left me to pick up Suzy's glove and hand it to him.

"He was just lucky," I said and moved quickly away.

The center fielder's prediction had been correct. Most Halos' batters came up two or three times as they scored fourteen runs in the bottom of the third. Mercifully, darkness set in and the game had to be called.

Dad was upset. "I was just finding my groove," he complained.

Jacqueline laughed and kissed him on the nose, which surprised me and surprised Dad a lot more. We had one beer at the post-game bash to be polite and then got the hell out of there. All of us, even Doug. As we drove away, I noticed Dad paying a lot of attention to our three fifty-six hitting second sacker.

On the way back to High River, where most of us had motel rooms, we stopped at a Chinese restaurant. Vince had recommended the place. It had all the ambience of a service station men's room. The owner had invested somewhere between eight and ten dollars on decor, mostly in the form of a few lanternlike objects made of what looked like crepe paper. These hung from the ceiling in a few locations.

To Vince's credit, however, the joint had the two things that were important to me. Good food and a telephone. I ordered and then headed for the phone. As I passed Dad and Jacqueline, they were giggling and coochy-cooing like a couple of eighth graders. It made me sick, but that might have been because I was jealous. The woman I wanted to coochy-coo was about to go live with a defensive back with only slightly more speed than the Halos' center fielder.

I hadn't talked to Angela for a few days, and I was really missing her. I dialed her number, fully aware that she had told me she was going to be away. My heart did a rap-song beat when someone picked up the phone.

"Hello." Either Angela had had throat surgery to make her sound like one of the Oak Ridge Boys, or it was not she who'd answered.

"May I speak to Angela, please?" I asked.

"Who's this?" asked the deep male voice.

"Who's this?" I countered.

"This is Angela's fiancé."

"Fiancé? Bullshit," I said loud enough to turn every head in the Golden Dragon or Silver Lantern or wherever the hell we were. "She never said she was going to marry you. And she's only going away with you out of pity because you're the worst defensive back in CFL history."

"Is this the asshole from the parking lot?"

"No, I'm talking to the asshole from the parking lot."

"Listen to me, you—"

That's as far as he got. The next voice I heard was a great deal more pleasant.

"Doc?"

"Yes it is."

"Why are you calling me?"

"Same ol' reason. I love ya to bits." I was ecstatic to hear her voice.

"But you can't do this. We said the other night that—"

"I changed my mind."

"What?"

"I changed my mind," I repeated. "I want to make love after all. Now."

"I'm sorry but that isn't possible. The . . . the offer's expired."

"Dennis doesn't sound like a very nice person."

"He says the same thing about you."

"I think you'll tire of him. Real fast."

"I don't think so."

I decided to change tactics. "I thought you said you were going away."

"I am. I was going to leave sooner, but I had to give a few days notice at the university, and I had some banking to do."

"Banking? You have money? You see . . . I was right. You don't need Dennis."

"I told you before it has nothing to do with money."

"Angela, can I just ask you one question? Have you thought about me at all these last few days?"

"I have to go now."

"Have you?"

"Yes . . . some."

"Well, I haven't stopped thinking about you at all. Not once. We played a baseball game tonight, and the whole time I was in the field, you never left my mind. Hell, I caught several line drives, stole a few bases, drove in God knows how many runs, and the whole damn time you were right there with me."

I had a good reason for lying about my accomplishments in the game. I figured any woman would be devastated if she thought the only athletes she could attract were ones without any actual athletic ability.

"How was the game?" she asked, though I knew it was more to avoid the real issue than out of genuine interest in my baseball fortunes.

"We romped," I lied again. "Listen, if I think about you all the time, and you think about me some of the time, then we must be getting close to the real thing, wouldn't you say?"

"No, Doc, I wouldn't say that. In fact, I'm not going to say anything more at all. I'm going to hang up now. Bye."

"I love you, Angela, and—"

She was gone. I hung up the phone and turned to walk back to the table. Every person in our group had been listening to my side of the conversation. As I looked at them, I detected sympathy on a couple of faces, cynicism on a few more and flat out incredulity on the rest.

"We romped?" Doug smirked.

I shrugged and sat down as a platter of ginger beef and pea pods arrived in front of me.

Across the table, Dad had his hand resting on Jacqueline's. "I guess I never really spent enough time with you on the subject of women, did I, son?" He winked at Jacqueline.

I passed him a bowl of deep fried pork. "Have some cholesterol, Dad. Have a bunch."

CHAPTER SEVEN

The next day we reshot the bull-riding segment, a day later than we'd figured. One thing I learned quickly about the movie business was that a schedule is a very tentative concept.

So at seven a.m., the morning after the ball game, my head feeling like a well-dribbled basketball, I looked in once more at Bucky Nichols as he tied himself on—the easy part—and summoned the courage—the hard part—to ride a bull called Lights Out.

I was familiar with this bull and knew that neither Bucky nor I could afford to make a mistake. The bull belonged to Rex Keller, the semi-congenial stock contractor I had bid my last farewell to in Medicine Hat. Rex was sitting on the fence, leering at me the way rodeo stock contractors do when they think one of their critters is about to dance the rumba on your rib cage.

"He'll make you wish you'd stayed in retirement, Doc," he called out.

"He's a pussycat," I told Rex. The statement reeked of false bravado. In fact, I felt that Rex had good reason for optimism.

I looked around to make sure everything was ready for the shot. I sure as hell didn't want to have to do this segment again. In the chute, Bucky was going through his pre-ride gyrations. I was more inclined to let him take his time this time around, mostly because I was in no hurry myself.

Eventually, though, Bucky nodded and the gate swung open. The bull went straight up on his first jump and came down hard on his front legs while kicking out his hind legs. Bucky was already in trouble. He'd been thrown forward and down on the bull's neck, and his face hit the bull with a smack like a beaver tail hitting water.

He surprised me though by making an effort to recover. He hung in there almost literally for maybe four seconds before Lights Out made a lawn dart of Bucky's body. The head-first landing has a tendency to stun a cowboy so I knew I'd better get in and take the bull out of there. I stepped in and let Lights Out see me, then moved away, leaving Bucky uninterrupted in his effort to sustain or regain, I wasn't sure which, consciousness. Things went pretty well right up until I stumbled just in front of the out gate and the bull. Lights Out had no choice but to hit me. He didn't do so out of any real malice, but that fact was of small consolation as our heads met.

A couple of scientific principals were at play here. The first is that a bull's head is considerably harder and heavier than a human's. The other has to do with things in motion striking things that aren't. The bull was moving at a good rate of speed. I was on all fours and immobile. The only happy part of the encounter was that my head fit perfectly between the bull's horns so all I got was skull.

Things got a little fuzzy after that. When I came to, I was lying on my back looking up into a mirror. Except it wasn't a mirror. It was Bucky, bandage on nose, his face pretty much an exact duplicate of mine. Lights Out, in what must be some kind of record, had broken two noses in about five seconds. His own nose came through the episode unscathed.

Bucky's face moved away and was replaced by my father's. He looked serious, and I prepared myself for the "Don't fight bulls on Tuesday" speech, although I wasn't certain what day we were dealing with at that exact moment.

"Son," my dad said, a little tenderly I thought for the start of the standard tirade.

"Dad?" I said.

"Jacqueline and I are going to be married. We'd like your blessing."

A cloud of cold black steam seemed to explode out of Dad's nostrils and closed over me before I had time to bless anybody. . . .

"She's a lot younger than you are, and you come from vastly different backgrounds." I rested my elbows on my knees and leaned forward, partly to convey earnestness and partly to keep from throwing up, an after-effect of my meeting with Lights Out.

The yawn overcame my father. We were sitting on a couple of borrowed lawn chairs not far from where the crew was filming an interview with an old-time bronc rider, a contemporary of Dad's. It was my first day back on the set. I'd been out of action for a couple of days, but except for a little bruising, which makeup could look after, my face didn't look too bad, much to the relief of Vince. He had visited me in the hospital during one of my lucid periods and waxed enthusiastic about the quality of the bull-riding sequence.

"It'll be one of the highlights of the show," he had beamed. "You were great."

Then he'd stared rather closely at my nose and the rest of my face, never once mentioning the concussion part of my condition.

As I looked at Dad, my head was still hurting, and it took a major effort to concentrate on the issue at hand.

"Mm-hmm," Dad fought off a yawn.

"I mean this is a woman who applauds the efforts of Greenpeace, and there's nothing wrong with that, but the only organization you ever belonged to . . . what was it? . . . The Don Cherry Society to Promote Violence in Hockey.

"Forgetting the ideological differences, what about the fact that you've known each other, what, six days?"

"Eight."

"Eight then. That's one day longer than a week."

"It's long enough when you get to my age," Dad shrugged. "I may not have time for a prolonged courtship, you know."

He had a point. "But—"

He waved both arms. "Let's not forget that I'm hearing all this from a guy who committed his life to somebody in a doggy costume after a half hour."

"That's different."

"Right. That's a half hour shorter than an hour."

"Well, at least I hope you're not planning to rush into the wedding thing. I mean there's nothing wrong with an extended engagement."

"We're getting married Saturday," Dad said.

"What day is this?"

"Monday."

"You're kidding, right? What was it, four or five days ago you couldn't stand each other?"

"Sure we disagreed on a couple of things, but she's a hell of a woman, Kid. One of the best I've ever known."

"That's great but—"

"The fact is I'm not really interested in what you think of my courting method . . . but I did want to talk to you about something. Something we probably should have talked about before, Dave, but I guess there never seemed to be a good time."

I couldn't remember the last time my dad called me by my name. For as far back as I could recall, I'd been "Kid," "Son," "Bucko" and a bunch of others I've forgotten.

Dad was staring at the rodeo arena. "You remember out at Cloverdale how I told you I'd been . . . getting together with Rhonda Rae. Well, you figured out it was a lie and said something about me being a nice guy."

Dad's voice was soft. I started to tell him that I'd meant what I said, but he held up his hand to stop me.

"You were wrong." He moved around on the lawn chair before he continued. "I wish I could tell you different but I can't."

"You don't have to do this, you know."

"Yeah, actually I do," he nodded and looked at the ground. "I wasn't always real good to your mom. I was never really there when she needed me. Most of the time I was away rodeoing . . . and as long as there've been rodeos, there've been gals like Rhonda Rae who really believe that one day they'll fall in love with a cowboy who'll love 'em back like they see in the movies. Only all they ever get, most of 'em, is screwed around by guys who can't hardly remember their names twenty minutes after the humpin's done.

"I was one of those guys. I'm not proud to say it, but I was. Before I met your mom . . . and after.

"The night your mom had the heart attack that . . . that took her, I was with somebody else, a woman I couldn't honestly describe for you right now.

"When I finally got to the hospital, I told your mom I'd been tied up at a meeting with a few guys from a rodeo committee that was thinkin' about hirin' me. I looked down at her. She was lookin' back at me, and she tried to smile, but I knew she knew. And a couple of hours later she died.

"The crazy part is . . . I loved that woman so much, you just can't imagine. Problem was I just never grew up. I was in my fifties and still wanting to act like a twenty-year-old stud even though the best woman in Canada was sitting at home waiting for me. Lots of nights your mom would give up waiting and go to bed before I got home, but you know something? She always left a note for me on the little table in the hall. Never once forgot to write that note, even though she had to know what kind of shit I was pulling.

"So I decided that night that since I'd never been faithful to your mom while she'd been alive, I'd be faithful to her after she was gone. And even though I don't suppose she can ever know one way or the other, I've never touched a woman since and didn't expect I ever would again. And it might surprise you to know that there's still a few opportunities out there for a guy like me." Dad wiped a sleeve across his nose. He stood up and walked a few steps away from me.

"So you see, Rhonda Rae and Mrs. Claysmore's younger sister, they were both safe as hell with me." He turned to face me with a half grin.

"But now I've met somebody, and it's a lot different than it was with any of those rodeo girls. Different than it was with anybody but your mom. What I wanted to ask you . . . do you think your mom would mind what I'm doing now?"

I detected a glistening in the eyes of this old man, who, though he was my father, was in many ways a stranger to me.

I looked down at the ground. I hadn't been trying to be a jerk. I just wanted my old man to be happy. Why couldn't they just take a little more time? On the other hand, how could I be sure that he and Jacqueline didn't feel about each other exactly the way I felt about Angela, as weird as some people thought that was.

I looked up at my father. "No, I don't think Mom would mind at all. And I know she'd approve completely of the lady you've chosen."

Dad reached down and put a weathered old palm against my face. We hadn't been the kind of people who did a lot of touching, and I couldn't honestly recall him ever doing that before.

"You really think she would?" He sat down again.

"I really do."

"Thanks, Kid."

"And by the way, I feel the same way myself. She's terrific."

"She is that, Son, she is that."

We sat for a while like that, neither of us wanting to end something that had taken over forty years to start.

"Can I tell you something now?" I said.

"Sure."

"You know how whenever you and me and Mom used to go places in the car or the truck, to rodeos or camping or whatever, you used to sing 'Don't Fence Me In'? Do you remember?"

"Hell, yes. I think it was the only song I knew all the words to."

"You wanna know something? When I'm driving now, going someplace and I'm all alone, a lot of times I'll sing that song."

He leaned forward and smiled at me. "It isn't a hell of a lot for a father to have given his kid, is it?"

"You gave me lots more than that."

"And now here's the both of us doin' our damnedest to get ourselves fenced in." He shook his head and smiled.

"Well . . . there's fences and there's fences." It was one of those things you say sometimes without knowing what it means or what is has to do with what's being talked about. I was glad Dad didn't bother to point that out.

"Haven't sung that song for a long time. Probably can't remember it anymore." He stood up then and rocked back on his heels. "Well, enough of this sentimental shit. Let's go get something to eat. By the way, now that I've got my own love life in order, maybe I'll have time to give you a hand with yours."

I wanted to say something smart, but I couldn't think of anything. Truth is, I probably couldn't do any worse with Dad's help than I had on my own.

CHAPTER EIGHT

I don't think it was entirely my fault as chief organizer that the wedding was . . . well . . . non-traditional. Doug said it was like a movie. One co-directed by Fellini and Disney. I felt that was a little uncharitable.

Jacqueline, who had never been married, wanted a small intimate wedding. Dad was into huge, garish, crowded and tasteless. He suggested we have it at the West Edmonton Mall. We compromised. A total of seven people were at the ceremony, but we had it in a church annex that could have comfortably housed the Grey Cup game.

The wedding party consisted of Jacqueline, Dad, Doug, who had made such an impression on Jacqueline that he was giving the bride away, my son Larry, the officiating minister, Vince and the best man— me. Vince, ever the sweetheart, had insisted on the crew having to do some night filming of a nearby rodeo, so none of them could come. Dad had invited the Halos, but they were attending a biker rally near Jasper. They sent their best wishes. Actually, they sent a message that said they hoped Dad got so much tail his dick would fall off, which was probably the Halo equivalency of best wishes.

Jacqueline wore a lovely off-white gown and a veil that cost two hundred and forty-five smacks. Dad wore a Denver Broncos sweatshirt and a sports jacket he borrowed from his landlord, who weighs two hundred and forty-five pounds. I thought that despite a ripped pocket and a couple of fairly inconspicuous cigarette burns, the groom's ensemble was fairly chic.

The minister, Reverend Hobnatz, told us he was an independent. Which means that he wasn't actually in charge of a church. After hearing his handling of the exchange of vows, I can understand why. He looked like he'd have been more at home in Jasper with the Halos, and his grammar included some innovative constructions. Among them, "Don't you, Jacqueline"—he pronounced it Jack Clean—promise that you won't never take no others?" The bride was understandably puzzled about how to correctly answer the question.

Later, the Reverend declared that ". . . what God has joined together let nobody take out from under us." And he finished in fine form with, "I now announce you a married husband and wife."

He forgot the "You may kiss the bride" part so Dad asked if it was all right.

"You wanna kiss 'er?" Reverend Hobnatz made it sound like the request of a pervert.

"It's sort of traditional," I interjected. I felt I had an obligation as best man.

"They do it at all the big weddings," Doug added.

"I s'pose," said Reverend Hobnatz.

Dad lifted Jacqueline's expensive veil, and they had just begun a tender kiss, the kind you see in old Cary Grant movies, when Reverend Hobnatz said, "That'll be forty-five bucks plus GST."

"We'll give you forty." Dad broke off kissing.

I leaned toward my father. "You don't haggle over price with a minister," I whispered.

"I did when you married Diane," Dad winked at me. "Got him down a few bucks, too."

While some might have considered the wedding a bit out of the ordinary, it was downright dull compared to the reception, but again I don't think all of the problems can be blamed on me. First of all, I had nothing to do with the double booking of the hall by the Job's Daughters Social Committee. And, if the Kingsland Rugby Club and assorted wives, girlfriends and retinue had been a little more cooperative initially, the thing could have worked.

We finally agreed to spit the hall down the middle. The rugby group of a hundred and thirty or so would have the north side of the hall, the seven members of the Allen wedding party the south half. Seemed simple enough to me.

The problem started with the music. We of the matrimonial group were small in number but mighty in decibels. Doug had one of the truly great stereo systems on the planet, the kind that at three-quarters volume could out-tweeter/woofer an entire regiment of jackhammers. Thus my Bon Jovi, Peter Gabriel and Tom Cochrane records were laying to waste the north side offerings of Tom Jones, Dionne Warwick and the like.

After a half hour or so, a couple of the rugby types crossed the center line to negotiate on this point. Doug offered to let them use his system for ten minutes out of every hour, and while this was being discussed, Dad made what I thought was a relatively inoffensive comment about the size and shape of the biggest guy's nose. The fight that ensued was brief and decisive.

Dad, Doug, Reverend Hobnatz and I were instantly surrounded by assorted props, hookers and wingers, and after maybe twenty seconds of action, Doug's Dennis Horner wound had been reopened, Reverend Hobnatz was doing the dead chicken on the floor, Dad was being held over the head of the guy with the large nose and I had managed to tunnel my way under a pile of bodies, which, given the range of possibilities, was not the worst position to be in. I never did figure out where Vince was while all this was going on.

After the fight broke up, if you can call what took place during the opening bars of "Green Green Grass of Home" a fight, Dad and Doug seemed a lot more open to negotiation, and we reduced Bon Jovi et al to a more acceptable volume level.

The rugby folks apparently harbored no ill feelings toward us and even helped revive the Reverend and halt the bleeding to Doug's mouth. Later in the evening, they passed the hat and during a rather regal moment, presented Jacqueline and Dad with the proceeds—thirty-seven dollars and sixty-eight cents, and a magnificent assortment of condoms, rugby players apparently holding the same sentiments about marriage as motorcycle gangs.

On the way home from the reception, my son Larry turned to me.

"I hear you're gettin' it on with Ralph the Dog."

I hadn't seen the kid in about three and a half months, and this was our first time alone. "News travels fast."

"Grandpa told me."

"Yeah, well, he got it wrong." I looked over at Larry. "I'm not getting it on with anybody."

"Too bad."

"There's worse things than not having a girlfriend," I said defensively.

"At my age maybe. At your age I'm not so sure."

Larry and I hadn't had a real discussion of anything since the night four years earlier when Diane and I sat him down to explain that we were splitting up.

"What's wrong with you people?" he had screamed. "We're a family. We've always been a family."

It was a long time before I realized that the kid had made the only truly sensible point in the whole discussion. Now he was thirteen and typical of his age. Precocious, bordering on obnoxious. Kind of a pain in the ass. But still making good points.

"So how do you like the guy your mom is marrying?"

"He's all right. Awful yuppy. They're always having people over who speak with accents."

"What's he do?"

"Eyes."

"What?"

"He's an eye doctor, but not just your ordinary optometrist. He's some kind of specialist."

"You . . . you and him do stuff together?"

"Sure. He's a real good golfer. He's teaching me."

I winced. I'd always wanted to teach my son to golf, but the truth was my own game was such a mess, I probably couldn't have taught him a damn thing.

"That's good," I said.

We drove in silence for a while. "You gonna play hockey this winter? Maybe I'll be able to get to some of your games."

"I don't know. Actually, I think I might start in gymnastics. And maybe Tai Kwan Do. I haven't decided yet."

"Sure, well those are good activities." I nodded so hard I hurt my neck.

We were almost to Doug's apartment. He wouldn't be coming home that night, having made a connection with a girl who worked for the outfit that was catering the film.

"Why don't you hang around for a few days?" I suggested. "We're almost finished shooting, and then you and I could grab a couple of days of fishing, or I could kick your butt around the golf course. What do you think?"

"Well, I don't know, Dad. I've got a couple of things on the go back home. And I'll be coming out again in a couple of weeks anyway. I'd kind of like to get back to my friends. We're planning a camping trip, you know, just guys, and I need to be there to help . . . and, well, to tell you the truth, rodeo doesn't really do it for me anymore, you know?"

"Sure, the camping thing sounds like fun."

Maybe he sensed my disappointment or maybe he figured a little time with the old man couldn't be that bad. Anyway, he said, "I could stick around for a couple of days though. See what's doin' with the movie business, and you and me can hang out some, is that okay?"

I reached over and mussed his hair, which wasn't easy. He had it cut so short it was like running your fingers over a hand-woven floor mat. We both laughed louder than we felt and stopped at a video store to pick up a couple of movies.

Larry went to bed after we had watched a *RoboCop* clone movie. I stopped counting corpses at fifty-seven. I might have missed a few in the blowing up of the Greyhound Bus scene. I can't actually remember the name of the movie, but I figure *Steel Dick* would be an all right title for a spin-off on the robot cop theme. It could also add some real interest to the sex scenes.

After Larry headed off to the sack with a Hardy Boys novel, something I could relate to, I sat in the dark and stared at the windows and balconies of the apartment across the street. I was beginning to wonder if my obsession with Angela was really just a desire for a second chance. A wish to replay the whole family thing and get it right this time. I didn't think that was it, but I couldn't say for sure. On the other hand, if that was the motivation, or even part of it, was that altogether bad? Not that any of it mattered anyway. It was clear that Angela had taken a place in the historical section of my life's card catalogue.

My concentration was diverted by the goings on at one of the third floor suites of the neighboring apartment. A girl and guy in what I'd guess was their early twenties, were doing a lot of huggy kissy stuff on the balcony. It was a hell of a lot more entertaining than the movie had been, probably because the scene on the balcony had some feeling to it.

After a while the girl went inside and flopped on a sort of bean bag chair. I could just see her if I leaned forward. The guy stayed on the balcony for a while and watched the traffic, then headed inside. I thought he was crazy to have given the traffic even a heartbeat of his time. As he was going by the bean bag chair, the girl reached up and pulled him down, wrapping her legs around him as he fell on top of her.

A minute of two later, he disengaged himself, went to the window and closed the curtains, no doubt to shut out prying eyes. Another minute or so went by, and the lights in the apartment went out. As I watched the lovers next door, I ached for the company of someone like the woman in the bean bag chair. I fantasized that maybe they'd have a fight, she'd throw the jerk out and at any second the phone would ring and it would be her.

"I couldn't help but notice you over there," she'd say. "You're a real man and all, so I got rid of El Wimpo in the hopes that you might share your body with me for the next seven or eight hours."

The phone rang. No shit, it did.

In my fantasy, the woman's voice had been husky, but the voice on the line was a little too husky.

It was Doug.

"What're you doin'?"

I was impressed by the fact that here it was after eleven p.m., and Doug wasn't even slurring yet.

"Oh, just catching up on my Shakespeare," I said. *"Romeo and Juliet,* the balcony scene. Great piece of theatre."

"I've got a better piece for you."

"What?"

"Dana has a friend, a cousin actually."

"Thanks, Doug, but I can't make it. Larry's sleeping and I don't want him to wake up without me here."

"The kid's thirteen."

"Yeah, I know, but I haven't exactly been around for him up to now, you know what I mean?"

"This is no dog, Dave . . . oh shit, I forgot, you're into dogs."

"Only one."

"She's foxy as hell. I'm serious."

I noticed Doug's description of women tended to involve members of the canine family.

"I appreciate the thought, Doug, I really do, but I can't."

"Okay, we'll come there. Just take a quick peek at my liquor supply. Make sure there's some vodka in there. Yours, her name's Christy, is a vodka drinker."

"Doug, I really don't think I'm up to—"

"Never mind. I know a bootlegger. We'll grab some on the way home. See you in half an hour."

He hung up and I sat for a long time, the receiver in my hand, staring at the darkened window of the apartment across the way. Somehow what Doug was proposing take place between someone named Christy and me wasn't in the same league with what was no doubt going on in that suite. It's not like I'd never had a one night stand before, but it just didn't feel right.

I was still sitting in exactly the same place when the trio of revelers arrived. Doug was holding a bottle of something in one hand and a plastic glass in the other. He had made a rapid advance toward the slurred speech stage.

"No problem ol' buddy," he assured me. "I was in the backseat. Christy did the driving."

As the introductions were being made, I had a good look at Christy. Doug had not overstated her physical presence. She was blond with wholesome pink cheeks and eyes that sparkled. I've read and heard about women with sparkling eyes, and I always thought it was crap. Harlequin romance stuff. The fact is, this woman's eyes sparkled.

She was smiling almost shyly as she held out her hand. I shook it and it was cold, or at least cool, probably from the chill of the night. I couldn't believe that anybody who looked or behaved like her could possibly have come from Doug's circle of acquaintances. I had been expecting something akin to the snoring redhead of a few weeks previous so Christy was a major surprise. Even Doug's date, Donna or Darlene or something looked reasonably civilized. I didn't get much opportunity to assess her as they headed for the bedroom almost immediately. This was probably good strategy on Doug's part because another half hour drinking whatever was in that bottle would have no doubt rendered him useless, romantically speaking.

Christy and I sat in the semi-dark of the living room listening to *American in Paris*—she chose the music—and drinking beer, Doug having forgot the vodka. For half an hour or so we did small talk and the obligatory exchange of life stories. I felt I should be honest with her.

"This evening is probably a waste of time for you," I said. "I'm sort of . . . committed to somebody."

"So you think your company is so dull that my night will be wasted if we don't screw, is that it?"

That wasn't what I had expected to hear. "Well, no but—"

"Doug told me about her. She's the one who does the mascot thing at the football games?"

"Yeah, well it's not a regular gig for her." I felt the need to explain. "She was just filling in."

"Doug said she's very special."

"He did? Doug said that? The guy who you drove over here tonight? That Doug?"

"Yes." She laughed a nice kind of laugh.

"I guess I've never heard Doug describe a female in those terms."

"We don't have to make love, you know. I mean it's fine with me if we just talk and visit. I don't think I share my cousin's hormonal imbalance."

"Your . . . uh . . . vocabulary is a little . . . uh . . . more extensive than a lot of Doug's nocturnal visitors."

She laughed again. It was neither an explosive blast nor a giggle. It seemed to come form her chest. It was the kind of laugh I bet a lot of women practice, but for Christy it was natural. "I'm in second year microbiology at Queens. Now if you really want some vocabulary, let me tell you about some of the organisms we've been studying."

I faked a yawn. "Will you look at the time? Damn, and I wanted to hear about those organisms, too."

She laughed and I laughed, and suddenly, quite by accident, I was having a good time.

We talked about family for a while. She thought my dad must be a lot of fun to be around. I guess he can be at times.

Christy pointed at the fireplace. "Does that work?"

"Yeah, sure," I said and got up to build a fire.

Neither of us spoke again until after the fire was blazing nicely.

"How old are you, Doc?"

"How old is your father?" I asked her.

"Forty-two or forty-three. I'm not positive."

"I'll be forty-two next month." I settled back in the chair. "It's a good thing we decided not to make love because it wouldn't have worked anyway. You'd feel like you were balling your dad, and I'd feel . . . old."

She set her beer down and came and knelt in front of my chair. Then she put her elbows on my thighs, leaned forward and kissed me. When I tell people what I'm about to say next, they usually brand me as a weirdo, maybe even a pervert, but the truth is, I keep a ratings list of every woman I've ever kissed. I wrote it out on the back of a cigarette package back in my smoking days, and I've kept it and revised it ever since. As Christy kissed me, I realized the list was going to require a major update.

She wasn't one of those women who slathered you with her tongue. She offered it, gave it, danced it around the inside of your lips, and then it was gone as if inviting you to come and get more. I went and got more. For several minutes I was kissing and being kissed by a Nobel Prize winning mouth.

"Gee, that's funny," she leaned back and smiled at me. "I didn't think about my dad once while we were doing that."

"Neither did I." I noticed my voice was sort of raspy.

"Do you feel old?"

"Hell, yes, at least twenty-seven."

"We could take this to the next step, you know." She undid the top button of my shirt and kissed my throat.

"I thought you said something earlier about being opposed to the idea." The kiss hadn't cured my rasp.

"I didn't say that. You did. I just said we didn't have to make love for my evening to be complete. Of course, it could be a little more complete . . . but I don't want to mess things up for you with your lady if you think—"

I put my index finger against her lips. "They're already messed."

Even as I said that, I wasn't sure I wanted to be with someone when I felt the way I did about Angela. I mean I wasn't stupid about it. I knew that Angela wasn't out there fighting off the advances of Dennis Horner so she could be true to her rodeo clown. But while what Christy and I were talking about doing didn't feel wrong, it didn't feel right either.

"Perhaps we could start out slowly. Maybe we could have a bath together," Christy whispered.

This created a new problem, well, two problems. One, I've always associated the pre-love making bath routine with Las Vegas call girls. Not that I have actual "hands-on" experience, but it's a perception I have, borne out by the morning after victory stories of assorted friends. Mind you, Christy did not look like any call girl I'd ever seen, even the Vegas variety, who are a classy looking lot.

Two, in spite of my checkered past, I am first and foremost a shy person. Especially about displaying the male part of my anatomy. It doesn't have to do with shame exactly. Discomfort might be a better word. I'm not totally comfortable in a society that puts a premium on performance and attaches unwarranted importance to the size of the male member.

Let's say I'm of average size. That means there are several million guys out there who are bigger. And I've always had this admittedly unjustified suspicion that women, especially women of the new morality, probably follow the advice contained in the slogan of a major supermarket chain: "Shop and compare." I know, I know, this from a guy who keeps a kissing rating list.

Christy managed to make me feel a lot less shy than usual. She was unhurried, remarkably natural. It seemed not to be a very big deal to her. This was something you did because you enjoyed it. Come to think of it, Diane had been a lot that way.

Mind you, I still turned my back to Christy while I dropped my jeans and shorts. But it wasn't long before we were up to our necks in suds and sipping glasses of a very nice German Reisling that I was shocked to find in Doug's fridge.

The chit-chat wasn't of the I-can-tell-a-kinkier-story-than-you-can variety. In fact, we discussed the topic that had been on my mind quite a bit of late . . . career choice. For probably twenty minutes, I rambled on. Christy listened and didn't stop me once except to fill my wine glass.

All my thinking on the subject had convinced me that my options were limited. One problem with devoting your entire life to perfecting one ultimately useless skill is that should the time ever come that you wish to diversify, you are somewhat hamstrung because you don't know how to do anything else. And there's damn little demand for forty-one year old ex-rodeo clowns. Other than in the occasional movie about ex-rodeo clowns.

As for my fledgling career as a writer, the more I thought about it, the more I realized it was a dream . . . a dumb dream. I was perfectly aware that writers with far greater talent and diligence than mine were stocking shelves in supermarkets and delivering pizzas.

I'd considered ending my brief retirement from rodeo. I have to admit that idea was mostly ego-based. I happen to believe I was very good at what I did. And Angela had never seen me work. I wished she had. I thought maybe if I came back and busted my ass for one more year, maybe I could get a last shot at a big one, maybe the Canadian Finals Rodeo, the end of season championship that takes place in the Northlands Coliseum in Edmonton. What the hell, I wanted to impress the woman I love. Is that so terrible?

Of course, deep down I knew I'd never get to work the finals. Not because I was older and losing my touch. Maybe I was, but that wasn't the reason. No, my biggest problem was that I was Canadian. And in rodeo, like so many sectors of the sports and entertainment industry in this country, we Canadians cling to that quaintly Canadian belief that American is better.

At Canada's biggest rodeos, most of the contract people, meaning clowns and announcers, have addresses on the south side of the forty-ninth parallel. I guess rodeo's like a lot of things in Canada. It's just a fact of life; we're an insecure people. So if the Finals was out, that left the Grimshaws of the world, and somehow I didn't think Angela would be all that impressed watching me slog around in the fifty centimeters or so of mud that usually occupies the rodeo arena in Grimshaw.

My un-retirement idea abandoned, I had tried to think of other possibilities. But the age thing kept coming up. The thing I like least about being over forty is that I'm not twenty anymore. I think maybe Yogi Berra said that. I'm not sure. He certainly could have.

Still, there had to be something I could do. Hell, I'd been to university. That had to count for something.

I take that back. If my time in university were the sole yardstick used, most people would justifiably conclude that I lack motivation, intelligence and all forms of mathematical skills.

Christy had a suggestion. "Let's look at it logically," she said between sips of wine.

As she was saying that, one of her nipples was winking at me through a gap in the suds, so logic was the furthest thing from my mind.

I resisted the temptation to reach out and fondle the round object that seemed to beckon me, and said, "Okay."

"Okay," she nodded. "Now you did two years of journalism school, right?"

I'd mentioned that during the life story exchange earlier. I now felt obliged to point out that during my second year of university, I had attended exactly four classes and passed, rather miraculously when you think about it, two courses, one of which was Introduction to Drama. So I was hardly qualified to be a journalist, although I did write for the school newspaper during my stay at Carleton. My articles were the usual student stuff—the administration sucks, the government sucks, the endless genuflecting of Canadian politicians toward their American counterparts sucks. Of course, all of this is true. It's just that none of it seems to matter as much once you're no longer attending university.

"Yeah, but still," Christy thoughtfully ran a bar of Zest across my chest, "you did study journalism and you did write for the newspaper and you do write poetry. And you want to write."

"Sure, and none of that will keep me and those I love from a lifetime of poverty. At some point, you have to know how to do something. Wanting it isn't enough."

"You know how to write so why don't you?" She looked at me with a naive confidence that instantly convinced me I could write the balls off Robertson Davies. "What sorts of things would you like to write?"

I shrugged an answer, which made some of the suds float off into the air. Doug walked into the bathroom and, without even a lifted eyebrow of recognition for the occupants of the bathtub, proceeded to urinate for what seemed like an excessively long time. When he had at last finished and left without flushing, Christy went on as if nothing had happened.

"Well, what do you like to read?"

I reached over and flushed the toilet. "I don't know, a little of everything, some classics, detective novels, westerns . . ."

"So why don't you write a western?" She got kind of animated with this new idea, and the winking nipple became positively agitated. "I bet you could write a terrific western. Who better to write a western than a cowboy?"

"Good point," I nodded, my eyes never leaving her bobbing breast.

"Or a detective novel. You'd be a fabulous detective story writer."

I noticed she hadn't suggested I pen a classic.

"Christy," I leaned back and looked at the ceiling, "it's really nice of you to think I should actually try to earn a living from writing. My dad suggested the same thing. Even tried to help me. But forget it. They haven't used a hundred words of what I've written for the film. And it's a western."

"That's different." She shook her head stubbornly. "It's not a real western. Not like Louis L'Amour or Zane Grey wrote. That's how I see you . . . as the next superstar of the western novel."

"What about poetry?" I teased. "Don't forget I've dabbled at poetry."

She wasn't about to be put off. "That, too. I bet you could. What we need is a plan. You must have a little money put away."

"'Fraid not. That's where the idea gets a little shaky. Other than what I'm making in this movie, I owe more than I've saved."

Which was true. If Diane hadn't been pretty decent about the child support during some of my non-peak earning periods, I'd actually owe her the money from this film and four or five more like it.

"Maybe you'll have to do something else for a while. Lots of writers have to do that. The thing is you're a writer so you should write when you can, and for a while you struggle, but then you make it and retire to one of the Gulf Islands with that woman of yours and some babies and a couple of dogs. It'll be great."

When she said the "great" part, she threw her arms up in the air and sent soap suds and water all over the bathroom. It all sounded so good when she mapped it out like that, and, best of all, she had a look on her face that told me she meant it. I actually began to believe her.

It was probably natural that a thought began sneaking around in my mind about this microbiology student with the sparkling eyes. Was she actually the woman I was supposed to retire to the Gulf Islands with? There wasn't anything clairvoyant about the thought. It was just a thought. Probably triggered by certain biological impulses taking place right about then.

She must have sensed what I was thinking because she shook her head and touched my face. "No, Doc, it's not me. There's somebody else the rest of your life is reserved for."

Then she grinned a wicked little grin and said, "Of course, that doesn't mean we couldn't have one fabulous night together, does it?"

I reached for that little space in the soap suds, and we didn't talk for a long while after that.

CHAPTER NINE

Christy was up and gone by the time I woke up, no doubt her thoughtful response to my expressed concern about Larry finding us together in the morning. She'd left a note on my pillow.

Doc,

You're terrific.

Write like crazy.

Love,

Christy

I pulled on a pair of sweatpants, poured a grapefruit juice and took up my position in the easy chair. For a while I studied the growing bulge of my stomach, something I swore I'd never let happen. As I did, a dream that I'd had that night suddenly came back to me.

In the dream I was old, even older than I am in real life, and I'd been standing at an intersection. I wasn't blind, but I couldn't see to get across the street. Christy was suddenly there and took my arm to help me across. She was wearing one of those harnesses like seeing eye dogs wear, but no leash was attached to it.

Angela was standing on the far curb but gave no indication that she was waiting for me. I'm not sure how I could tell that, considering I couldn't see, but a lot of what happens in dreams doesn't make sense. We were about halfway across the intersection when the light changed, and cars were zipping by in every direction. Most of the drivers were faceless, but I recognized a couple of people I knew. Tub Willoughby was driving a Volkswagen, and he grinned and waved as he went by. Stan Shofner was at the wheel of a farm grain truck, and only some quick action by Christy saved me from being mowed down by the son of a bitch.

Then a traffic cop materialized from wherever dream people come from, and she was yelling at us to get the beep out of the way. Really. The expletive was replaced by the sound of a beep. I looked at the traffic cop, for some reason I could see again, and the traffic cop was Diane. She was yelling some more stuff, this time about how I'd messed up my life at a beeping intersection just like this one years before, and here I was doing it again. Over her left shoulder, I noticed Stan Shofner had turned the grain truck around and was heading straight for us. Except it wasn't Stan Shofner anymore. It was Dennis Horner.

I must have woke up then because I couldn't recall anymore of the dream. For a while I tried to figure out what it meant, but deep thinking was out of the question that early in the morning so I resumed the contemplation of my swelling midsection.

Doug stumbled into the living room, clad only in shorts, sank down into the sag of the couch and grinned at me. He seldom did that, especially after a night of drink and real or attempted debauchery, so I figured something might be up.

"I am officially in love, ol' buddy," he said.

Doug had made that statement a minimum of once a month for as long as I've known him, which is going on a quarter of a century. That makes approximately three hundred professions of love, which explains why I didn't react to the latest announcement with the degree of enthusiasm he felt would be appropriate.

"Must be something in the water." I didn't look up. "A lot of people seem to be doing that falling in love thing. Or maybe it's a phase of the moon."

"I'm serious this time."

"Dora, was it?"

"Dana."

"Ah, Dana."

"She's a sensational broad. No, let me rephrase that. She's a sensational lady. And she's got the two things I've been looking a long time for in a woman."

"Let me guess, a six figure savings account and a belly button that hums 'Unchained Melody' during foreplay."

"Not funny. Not this time. Nope, the two things are she's crazy about me and she's crazy about making love."

I thought about that and realized there are worse criteria on which to base a long-term relationship.

"So does this mean you're going to see her again?" I was having trouble controlling my cynicism.

"Are you kidding? I'm trying to tell you this is the big one."

"If you tell me you're getting married Saturday, I'm going to slash my wrists."

"Maybe not Saturday, but I wouldn't rule out wedding bells for the old Douger at some point."

"Did you guys talk about age difference at all?"

"Sure, and Dana said if it worked for Trudeau, it can work for us."

"It didn't work for Trudeau. His wife ran off with a Rolling Stone or somebody."

"That wasn't because of his age. It was because of his job. And what about your dad?"

"He's been married less than twenty-four hours. Even Elizabeth Taylor's marriages last that long."

"You're a real pain in the ass sometimes."

I couldn't think of anything more to say so I sighed and looked over at the apartment across the way. I wondered if the guy and girl from the night before were up yet.

"Come on, man!" Doug's voice crashed in on the thought. "Just because things aren't going so hot in your love life, you could be happy for me couldn't you?"

"Okay, I'm sorry. I'm happy for you. Congratulations. Now shut up. I have to drink my juice."

"By the way, what'd you think of Christy?"

I didn't get a chance to answer because Larry padded into the living room and without greeting either Doug or me turned on the *RoboCop* movie for another go round.

As the opening scene's violence erupted on the screen, Doug said, "Awright!" and I headed for the bathroom to take a shower.

CHAPTER TEN

One of the recollections I have of my dad from when I was a kid is of him bringing home various and sundry individuals for dinner. This was done usually without notice, a fact that my mother displayed extraordinary patience with. The guests were, for the most part, of a class of people that nobody except for my father and maybe the Salvation Army would have cared to share a table with.

My dad rodeoed. But I don't ever remember breaking bread with a world champion bronc rider or the winningest calf roper on the circuit. No, the guys Dad brought home were generally those who hadn't won anything in the last three years and appeared not to have changed their clothes since they had last won. These vagabond visitors shared another trait, however. They were, in short, colorful. Each was without doubt a character, an original. My dad could attract interesting people, there was no mistaking that.

And he wasn't one to let the breaking-in period of something like a marriage interfere with a lifelong habit. So the day after he and Jacqueline were wed, the honeymoon having been put off until we finished the film, Dad brought home the first, for Jacqueline, dinner guest, another of his former rodeo cronies.

The man's name was Old Jake Bowlen. The "Old" part wasn't a throw-in like when we say, "You should've seen Old Harry last night. Got so drunk he threw up in the back of Old Frank's Mazda." The "Old" in Old Jake was official, like Bobby in Bobby Sue or Billy in Billy Joe. Which raised the question, had he been called Old Jake when he was a baby?

He hadn't been a baby for sixty-five to seventy years, I figured. He wasn't a big man, but you couldn't tell if he'd always been small or if he was in the process of shrinking as he got older. Wizened is the word that described him as well as any. Especially his face, which had a lot of permanent creases in it. He had the look of a Shih Tzu. An old sad Shih Tzu. He was wearing a suit, a brown three-piece suit, not exactly fashionable and probably very hot for August, and a brown stetson. The cowboy boots were the pointy toe kind that had been out of fashion since long before John Travolta rode all those battery powered buckers back in the seventies. And Old Jake chewed something that no one, not even Dad, had the courage to accept when it was offered.

Still, the old gentleman was that, a gentleman. Not from the modern era, no. Maybe not even from this century, but he had a quality about him that drew you to him. To listen, to watch. Maybe even to admire.

"Old Jake used to ride broncs back in the forties and fifties," Dad grinned at Jacqueline and me as he introduced the new arrival. "He was finishing up his career as mine was getting going. He's got a spread across the line in the Montana foothills just outside of Havre. He's the second generation of Bowlens on the place. It's just him and his son there now."

Old Jake had a son. I thought about that. There are people you meet in this life, and you say to yourself, this person has never been without his long underwear in mixed company. Old Jake was such a man. That he had a son meant that at some point in history, at least once, a member of God's most romantic species, woman, had been bedded by the man, Old Jake. Maybe she'd even become Mrs. Old Jake.

I wondered what Old Jake's offspring was called. Was he Young Jake or maybe New Jake? I made a mental note to ask first chance I got.

Dad was still grinning. "Old Jake heard they were making a movie about me and came up to say hello. He'll be staying for dinner."

It was several minutes before Old Jake spoke. This was due in part to the fact that Jacqueline had led Dad to the area behind the motor home I'd brought in for their privacy, and the two of them were engaging in what the politicians like to call a frank discussion.

I heard only one phrase ". . . something nice for the two of us," but that gave me a pretty good idea of what was being discussed. They returned minutes later, hand in hand, and I assumed that the first domestic crisis of their married lives had been resolved.

"I hope you like pot roast, Mr. . . . ."

"Bowlen," Dad filled in.

"Mr. Bowlen," Jacqueline smiled. "We're having pot roast, and we'd so like you to stay."

"Water," Old Jake said.

"Excuse me?" Jacqueline said.

"Water . . . everywhere." The old man waved an arm in a gesture that must have meant "everywhere."

Dad was smiling at Old Jake, and Jacqueline was looking questioningly at Dad. Which I couldn't blame her for. I mean, water, water, everywhere, is an odd response to "Do you like pot roast?"

"What . . . exactly . . . do you mean by that, Mr. Bowlen?" I asked.

"I grew up just west of here," he pointed. "In nineteen and twenty-three, I was six years old, damnedest flood you ever saw. All this was covered in water," he waved again. "The Highwood, she burst like a woman giving birth, and all the buildings in town were almost up to their windows in water. I remember my dad rowing me down main street to the barber so's I could get my hair cut. Life goes on even in a flood. Pot roast's fine."

I immediately recognized that Old Jake Bowlen—I'd been wrong in my estimate, he was seventy-four—was exactly the kind of person my father had always been attracted to. Dad probably even appreciated the bursting woman simile, which I had found a bit graphic. Not to mention inaccurate. In all my perusal of the tabloid titles while standing at the supermarket checkout, I had never once read, "Woman Bursts in Child-birth, Baby Lands on Nearby Lawn." Nevertheless, I figured Old Jake was going to be an interesting way to pass an evening.

He was, however, a pump that needed priming. Apparently fearful of dominating the conversation, Old Jake had to be prodded before he'd launch into a story. I wanted to ask him about prairie fires, the subject always having intrigued me. Recalling that the mention of pot roast had triggered the flood yarn, I wasn't sure whether I should approach the subject of prairie fires directly or come at it by mentioning a food group. I opted for the former.

"I'd bet you remember some pretty incredible prairie fires, eh, Mr. Bowlen?"

"You'd win," he said.

"Uh . . . yeah." I looked at Dad, but he wasn't looking at me. "Would you like to tell us about any . . . that . . . stand out in your mind?"

"Summer of nineteen and ten," he answered.

"Oh," I said and did a little quick mental math. I calculated that dur-ing the fire of nineteen and ten, Old Jake was minus seven years old. I began to think maybe I'd made a bad choice of topics.

"Course, I wasn't there. My dad told me about it," he began, my faith in the old man's memory restored. "Burned from below the Montana border pretty well all the way to Calgary. Homes burned, cattle, lots of other animals, the wild ones, too. When the wind blew, you couldn't outrun it. She burned the whole summer long."

"How'd they finally put it out?" Jacqueline asked.

"Didn't." Old Jake pulled out a pipe and a pouch of tobacco. He moved slowly, deliberately, to heighten the dramatic effect of his tale.

"It went out by itself when winter set in," he said when the pipe was finally puffing to his satisfaction. "Only thing that could stop the fire."

He was warmed up now and the fire story went on for another ten minutes. I wasn't sure if any or all of it was true, but it didn't matter. Nor did it matter that it probably differed with each telling. He enjoyed telling it, and I had to admit I'd enjoyed hearing it. We all had. And as the evening's dark began to close in around us, and the air cooled and the stars began their night dance overhead, that was enough.

The two older men wandered off to smoke and chew and spit and talk, leaving Jacqueline and me to set the table. I hadn't planned to stay, but Larry had gone golfing with Doug, and now that Old Jake was to be a part of the dinner party, I didn't decline when Jacqueline laid out four plates.

"You worried at all about setting a precedent?" I began setting utensils at the four places. "Pot roast, one of Dad's unique friends invited to dinner . . . all this on the first full day of your married life?"

"No," Jacqueline handed me cups and saucers, "I don't think so. When we went behind the motor home, I explained to him that from now on I want to know when guests are coming, in advance. And as for the cooking, we'll be sharing that and a lot of other things, too."

It wasn't a strident pronouncement but a simple statement of a fact.

"So you didn't momentarily lose your senses and your heart to the colorful cowboy?"

"Coffee?"

"Sure, thanks." I accepted a cup as Jacqueline sat down opposite me.

"Doc, I want you to know something. I did lose my heart, sort of, but not my senses. Not at all. I think in many ways this is the most sensible thing I've ever done." She poured cream in her cup, and we both watched it curl around in aimless circles.

"There seems to be a feeling that because I did some work for Greenpeace and that I come from British Columbia, I must be a card-carrying, head-in-the-clouds Bolshevik."

"Pretty well summarizes my perception," I said.

Jacqueline laughed and sipped the coffee. "Don't get me wrong. I was staunch NDP when I was in university."

"Weren't we all?"

"But I'm really pretty traditional in a lot of ways." She leaned in to me. "I voted for Vander Zalm for God's sake."

"No!" I covered my mouth. "Well, that at least explains why you married my dad. He represents tradition. And," I lowered my voice, "he reminds you of Bill Vander Zalm."

"Not exactly." She laughed again. "I know it'll sound silly if I tell you I love him, so I won't. I admire him, I like him a great deal. I think he's handsome, even sexy, and a lot more intelligent than he likes anyone to think . . . and once you get past the outer layer of bullshit . . . he's someone I enjoy being with."

"A couple of weeks isn't much time to figure all that out."

"No, it isn't. But I figured it out just the same."

"Do you like vacuuming?"

"What?"

"My old man hasn't vacuumed a single dust bunny in his whole life. When it comes to machines that suck up dirt, he's a virgin. Damn creative with the excuses though. The noise hurts his ears, the dust bothers his allergies, it hurts his back to bend over."

"He will vacuum, trust me."

I was developing new respect for my stepmother. "You've never been married?"

"No." There was a trace of something in her voice, not sadness exactly, but something.

"Why is that? I mean, I hope I'm not prying, but I find it hard to believe."

"Not that hard to believe really. Your father was the first man who ever proposed to me when he was stone cold sober."

"So . . . do you love him?"

"I don't know if I love him today, right this minute." She poured us more coffee. "But what I feel for him is close enough that it will become love if we give it a little time."

"You wouldn't care to tape that last statement and let me play it for the benefit of a certain woman in my life would you?"

"How's that going anyway?"

"I'd say it's gone. At least a ninety percent chance that it's over. And that might be a bit optimistic."

"That's too bad. I'm sorry."

"Yeah, well, it's my own fault." I tried to smile at her. "I never proposed to her when I was stone cold sober."

The pot roast was world class. And, the conversation was interesting, although perhaps a touch inappropriate. Dad got Old Jake going on famous murders of the area. We heard about a guy who shot-gunned his wife to death, two brothers who dueled it out with pitchforks, a dispute over sausage, I think it was, and my personal favorite, the story of the Lost Lemon mine.

"There's two camps on the Lost Lemon," Old Jake told us over the Apple Crisp that followed the main course, "them that believe and them that don't. Me, I'm a believer."

"It's in the mountains not that far west of here that the mine's supposed to be located. Two fellas, Lemon and Black Jack, had the gold, and they was bringing some of it out for assay. Greed overtook Lemon, and he hatcheted Black Jack to death one night. But then guilt set in, and he went bonkers and could never find the place again."

"They say there's an Indian curse on the whole area now. All kinds of stories of what's happened to them that's tried to find the mine. Nobody's succeeded of course."

When we'd finished the crisp and the two old-timers had smoked some more, I began hinting to Old Jake that maybe he and I should amble along and leave the newlyweds to themselves. The hints were lost on him, and finally it transpired that he would occupy the chesterfield of the motor home, Dad's suggestion, to which Jacqueline and I rolled our eyes.

I said my goodnights and headed for the GMC. As I looked back, I could see Dad with an unhappy look on his face, tying an apron around his waist in preparation for dish duty.

It hadn't been a bad evening, not bad at all.

CHAPTER ELEVEN

I wasn't kidding when I told Christy I hadn't done much writing for the show. In fact, my contribution hadn't gone much beyond the elimination of the "buckaroos" and "yippees" from Jacqueline's early attempts.

I had to admit that she was extremely professional, and most of what she wrote didn't need a whole lot of help from me. When additional scripting was required, Vince, not surprisingly, went directly to Jacqueline. And while my newest relation was the most cooperative woman imaginable and would have been happy to work with me, the simple truth was that I'd been kept too busy in front of the camera to be available for much of the writing.

But now, with only three or four days of shooting remaining to be done, my scenes were finished. The last stuff to be shot would actually be the first part of the film and would deal mainly with the history of rodeo. I hoped to finally get the chance to do some serious writing.

Jacqueline and I met early the next morning to discuss the remainder of the script. She stepped quietly out of the motor home with her laptop computer and her finger to her lips to indicate Dad and Old Jake were still sleeping. We set ourselves up at a picnic table, with Jacqueline at the computer and me with a notepad, cowboys being a little slow adapting to the new technology.

"I talked to Vince a couple of days ago," Jacqueline said. "The approach he wants to take is that rodeo is a natural extension of everyday activity on the ranch."

"Tricky in that we're dealing with fiction if we do that."

"What do you mean?"

"Rodeo, at least some of it, is an extension of the way things used to be on ranches. It's a reflection of the old days, with not a lot of connection to today's ranches. Take calf roping, for instance."

"Okay."

"Well, in the old days, calves were roped so they could be branded or doctored, just like Dad said during that first argument you two had. Today, a few ranches do things the traditional way, but there's a hell of a lot more that are into squeezes and snowmobiles and quads. Not exactly nineteenth century, is it?

"How about bronc riding?"

"It's probably the closest thing to what really took place on the old ranches. The early cowboys had to be good horsemen because they broke the horses they used for their daily work. And naturally enough, I suppose, they were also competitive. The top gun on one ranch would challenge the best rider on a neighboring ranch, and they'd ride the rankest toughest horses they could find."

"So maybe what we should be talking about is the natural extension of what ranching was."

"That's my point," I nodded. "But even there we've got a problem. bareback riding, steer wrestling, bull riding and barrel racing are spectator competitions pure and simple, and damn good ones if you ask me. And they're often performed by competitors who've come off the ranch. But that's where the extension ends."

"So what do we do?"

"I've always been a big believer in the truth," I said.

"Novel idea," Jacqueline laughed, "but hardly fashionable. Do you think it'll work with Vince?"

"It might," I said. "Vince wants to do a positive piece about rodeo. So do you and I. I just don't think we have to BS people to get it done. Rodeo PR types have been doing that for years."

"You know, I think you'd be the best one to write this section. They're planning to have your dad narrate it with some footage of rodeos and ranches in the background."

"Good idea," I agreed. "I mean the way they're planning to show it, not the me writing it part. Are you sure that—?"

"I'm sure," she put her hand on my arm. "Go ahead and do it. I'll be there to help or read or whatever you want me to do."

I'd only been at it about a half hour when Dad burst out of the motor home and, clad only in shorts, he rushed up to where I was working.

He grabbed my shoulder. "Where's Jacqueline?"

"I don't know. In the arena, maybe. What's up?"

"I gotta get her." He started off in the direction of the arena.

He stopped and looked back at me. I flicked my eyes in the direction of his underwear.

"Oh, yeah." He changed directions and ran for the motor home. "Do me a favor will you, Dave? Go get her. I'll get dressed and meet you back here in a couple of minutes."

I wasn't happy about being interrupted, but the sense of emergency surrounding Dad's erratic behavior had a ring of authenticity so I closed the notebook and went in search of Jacqueline. I found her talking to one of the sound guys, and we were back at the picnic table before Dad.

"What's going on?" Jacqueline questioned when we were once again seated.

"I don't honestly know. Dad's carrying on like there's some damn tragedy happening, but—"

I didn't get any further because at that moment Dad emerged once more from the motor home. This time he was fully clad, and his hair was even combed.

Jacqueline and I turned to face him as he hustled up to us.

"Okay, Dad, what's the big crisis?" For a second it occurred to me that this might be one of his elaborate and childish pranks a la the Cloverdale horse tail incident, but my father wasn't that good an actor. Something was definitely bothering him.

"It's Old Jake." Dad circled the table but didn't sit.

"What? Is he sick?" Jacqueline sat up sharply.

"Naw. Worse than that. He's about to lose his place."

"What do you mean?" I'd known Dad to misunderstand things in the past. I figured this might be one of those times.

"They're takin' his place. That's what I mean," he snapped at me.

"Could you calm down, Dad?"

"And sit down," Jacqueline added.

"Yeah, the circling is giving me a headache."

"He told me over coffee this morning." Dad didn't sit, but he did stop circling. "They haven't been able to make the payments for the last year, and the bank's takin' it over. Tomorrow afternoon. Four o'clock. The banker's coming with the sheriff. They're putting Old Jake and his son off the place . . . for good."

"That's awful," Jacqueline said. "Can they do that?"

"It's the goddamn way things are going in this world. The people that control the money can do anything they want to the little people."

"But you did say he hadn't been paying what he owed," I pointed out.

"Sure, but who's fault is that? You can't make a living in agriculture anymore, and any money you do make is taxed away from you. It ain't any better down there in the States than it is up here."

"Why would he have a mortgage anyway?" I asked. "You said his ranch had been in his family for a couple of generations."

"I don't know for Christ sake. Maybe he had to refinance. Maybe he bought more land. The point is are we going to help a friend or not?"

"Well, of course we want to help," Jacqueline nodded, "but what do you think we can do?"

"We go there tomorrow, and when the banker and the sheriff show up, we don't let them on the place. We send 'em packing."

"Oh, good idea, Dad," I snorted. "Then we spend six months or so in an American jail, and Old Jake loses his place anyway, but at least we've made a statement. And let's not forget that in the States damn near everybody carries a gun. We could get shot."

"You got a better idea?"

"A better idea would be to mind our own business," I said. "You make these guys sound like the Sheriff of Nottingham and Prince John, and we're Robin Hood and the boys taking from the rich to give to the poor. They're people just doing their jobs. It's the way the system works. You owe money, you pay."

"Bullshit!" Dad fell back on the method of arguing he was most comfortable with.

"But it doesn't seem right, Doc," Jacqueline interjected. "To let that poor man lose his land and his livelihood. Surely there's something we could do."

"What was to be done should have been done a long time ago," I countered. "The man should have paid his bills."

Dad stood up and leaned over the table until his face was whisker-burn close to mine. "You know something? You don't know squat about a lot of things, and this is one of them. I'm talking about friendship here, about helping somebody who needs it because he's your friend, not looking for some excuse to turn away from the guy. Sure he should've paid his goddamn bills, and he would've too if he could've, but he couldn't. He tried to talk to the banker, and the guy wouldn't listen. So now they're taking his place away. Except they're not."

Dad's voice got quieter. "Because I'm gonna be there and anybody else who wants to help, and we'll run those bastards off, and at the end of the day, Old Jake and his son are going to sleep in their own house."

"Look, I like Old Jake as much as—"

"Like hell you do!" Dad thundered. "I saw how you looked at him, like he was something on the bottom of your boot. Like you look at lots of people who either aren't weird enough or are too weird to meet your standards. Like you've looked at me lots of times. Don't think I haven't noticed. Well, there's something else you don't know shit about—"

"It was 'squat' before," I interrupted.

"Shut up! And it's about time you learned. You want to be a writer? . . . a storyteller? That man" he gestured in the direction of the motor home, "is a storyteller. You could learn a hell of a lot from him."

I don't know a lot about blood pressure, but I suspected my dad's was right up there. I was getting a little hot myself. "I heard his stories, thanks. I was here, remember, and I've had all the flood of nineteen and whatever, and hatchet murder yarns I need for a while."

"You be here tonight, right here. I'll have Old Jake here when we're finished shooting for the day. I want him to read to you from some of his notebooks. I want you to hear—"

"I have a date tonight."

"Bullshit! You're just afraid. Yeah, afraid of hearing somebody's words who actually has something to say. Besides, nobody'd date you. Women hate gutless men." He started to leave but stopped and turned back. "Just be here."

His face and voice softened as he faced Jacqueline. "My dear, would it be all right if I invited Old Jake and his son to be our dinner guests this evening?"

"That would be fine," Jacqueline smiled at him.

"And I hope you'll forgive my language. The boy got me riled."

He turned a second time and stalked off in the direction of the motor home, then changed his mind and headed out across the large field that ran along the west side of the rodeo grounds.

I looked at Jacqueline and rolled my eyes. "Back straight, shoulders back. You'll learn that that's Hoot Allen's body language for self-righteous indignation."

She didn't answer and avoided meeting my eyes.

"Oh, no," I said, "not you, too. Just what I need. Don Quixote and his wife tilting endlessly at windmills for the betterment of mankind."

I picked up my notebook and started for the pickup. I could feel myself getting angry, but I wasn't sure why or who I was angriest at. The warm time between my father and me had been short-lived, and I had to admit I liked it better when we got along. But this seemed so stupid, so futile. I couldn't go along with all his whims just to keep peace. I got to the truck and looked back as Jacqueline was stepping into the motor home.

Another thing that made me mad. I could have had a date. He shouldn't have assumed it was out of the question.

I spent the afternoon in a Chinese café in High River, the same one we'd gone to after the baseball game. I ate one egg roll, drank seven cups of coffee, went to the john four times and wrote not one word in my notebook, though it sat open in front of me the whole time.

I timed my arrival back at the grounds to miss supper. I hadn't been invited anyway. By the time I got there, Dad had Old Jake installed in a lawn chair near a respectable looking campfire.

"Right there." Dad indicated he wanted me to sit on a stump right across from Old Jake. Dad looked calm, almost friendly, and Jacqueline smiled and handed me a cup of coffee.

Another man was sitting near Old Jake and drinking a bottle of coke. I took him to be Old Jake's son.

"This is February," Dad announced, pointing at the man who as near as I could guess was about my own age.

I looked questioningly at Dad. "Without giving the impression that it is either too weird or not weird enough, may I ask if that is a name?"

"He was born then," Old Jake said as if calling somebody February was a perfectly normal practice in the field of baby naming.

"Sure," I said. "Glad to meet you, February. I met a fella from down your way once. You might know him. Name's Nineteen Thirty-Seven?"

That one got by the youngest member of the Bowlen family, but Dad caught it and scowled at me.

"Old Jake's brought along some stories. There's one or two I'd like you to hear," he said.

To be honest, I was surprised that Old Jake wrote his stories down. I thought he'd be the type to follow the oral storytelling tradition. Jake looked at Dad and seemed a little puzzled about what was expected of him.

"Go ahead, tell him the rodeo story." Dad pointed at the notebook Jake was holding.

Notebook is a little generous in describing the conglomeration of paper, pieces in every size and shape, that formed a pile on Old Jake's lap. He pulled out a tin of the substance he chewed, took a pinch, and passed it to Dad and February, both of whom declined with thanks. Then Old Jake selected, randomly it seemed to me, a piece of paper.

For twenty minutes or so he read, never fumbling the paper, never missing a beat. You had to listen hard to get it all. The old voice was tired and worn. But it spun a soft web that bound me irresistibly into it for as long as Old Jake spoke.

"'Midnight,'" he began, "the story's called 'Midnight.'"

One boy was city. One was country. He was Tom. He was Cody.

The last bull had been bucked maybe two hours before, and the two boys, cousins they were, sprawled in well-traveled lawn chairs. The country boy was the son of a rodeo stock contractor. The other, the boy from the city, had seen more skyscrapers than bucking horses. Gangly, messy-haired, dusty and tired. Both of 'em. The way boys are meant to be after a rodeo.

Tom was sleeping. Cody almost was. Or maybe neither of them was. Otherwise how would they, how could they have heard the fireplace-crackle invite in the voice of the old man. The old man with the bronc-stomped hat and the teeth that weren't all there, or if they were, they weren't in their proper places.

But they did hear him. And they answered. Cody first, "What d'ya want?"

Then Tom. "Do we know you?"

"I know you," the old man said, dragging a gnarled hand over a face that had long been unacquainted with a razor.

"I saw you ride that steer today," he said, pointing at Cody, "and you were on the fence." He pointed at Tom.

Tom swallowed. City boys know better than to talk to strangers, even if they're old.

Cody talked to everybody, didn't matter. "How'd ya like my ride?"

"Good enough." The old man took a package of snuff from the back pocket of his jeans. It was a brand neither of the boys recognized, and the jeans weren't the kind rodeo cowboys wore.

"You a cowboy?" the country boy asked him.

Tom covered his mouth with his hand. It was a joke, a little fun at the old man's expense, he knew. But the old man seemed not to notice. He looked across at the empty arena.

"Funny thing, a rodeo arena," he said. "Like a moment in time. Two, maybe three days a year it's alive, makin' history. The rest, it's gatherin' strength, restin' up for the time it kicks up life like dust under a fast horse's hooves." He wasn't talking to them now. They knew that. He was just talking. Suddenly, the old man with the out-of-place hat—it was felt and these were straw hat days—fascinated them.

And they looked at each other, and one shushed the other and then back the other way, and they listened the way boys listen, city or country, elbows on knees, shoulders hunched forward, eyes searching the road-map face.

Where was the wind? It had been there. But not now. No noise save the breathing and the words of the old man.

And the dark, too. It had fallen fast. Faster than usual.

"Take this arena here, for instance," the old man said. "Plenty of history between them fences. Some good history, some bad. Like boys in that respect, eh?"

He winked at them and began walking toward the arena. They followed. Boys will follow a good story anytime. Especially country boys. And city boys will follow country boys. They stayed close together and a respectable distance behind the old man who never once looked back to see if they were there.

He pointed. "Announcer's stand," he said. "A lot of people only watch what's happenin' in the bucking chute or in the arena. Big mistake. I like to watch the announcer's stand and clowns' trailers and the crowd. Watchin' those things, lot of times you know what's goin' on without ever lookin' at the men out there."

Cody couldn't see that and said so.

"Look there, now," a crooked finger pointed.

The announcer's stand was a dark shadow keeping watch over the rest of the sleeping grounds.

Tom saw it first. "Geez, Cody, what's happening?"

"I don't know." Cody blinked and watched.

Light was what was happening. Creeping, growing, building-in-strength light. First the announcer's stand, then the chutes and then the whole arena, all of it now in half-shadow.

A voice said, "I wanna welcome you boys. Special howdy to ya."

The voice was high-pitched and nasal with a hint of western twang. It was amplified over a loudspeaker that crackled like the boys' Grandma's old radio.

The voice was all rodeo. The old man pointed again, and now a pixie face could be seen peeking out of the announcer's stand and grinning friendly right at them from over an ancient microphone.

"That's Warren Cooper. You can't hardly see him 'cause he's short and he's ornery, but he's the best there is."

"Don't get smart with me, Gabe Pauley," the speaker crackled in time with the voice.

The old man laughed and shook a fist at the man in the announcer's stand.

"I remember," Cody blinked but didn't stop looking at the announcer's stand. "I remember going to the Calgary Stampede when I was little, and it was him I heard. When we were getting our popcorn and weren't even to our seats yet, it was him . . . but if that's Warren Cooper . . ." Cody looked at Tom and then at the old man.

"He's dead," the boy said, his voice an out-of-air whisper. "He died two, three years ago. I know 'cause my dad went to the funeral."

"Yep, and at a real good age, too. Damn near ninety," Gabe Pauley spoke louder then, "which qualifies him as an old crock, an' I hope ya heard me."

"I heard ya," the face at the microphone chuckled, "but I ain't got time to be tradin' insults with broken down sodbusters the likes o' you." Then the laugh in the voice was gone, and it dropped down like he was talking only to them. "It's time, Gabe, boys."

"Time?" Tom turned to the old man. "This is awful spooky mister. I think I'll be going."

He started, hoping that Cody would follow, but the country boy's boots moved the wrong way, toward the arena and up the fence, and then Cody was perched atop and lookin'. Lord, how he was lookin'.

"Cody?" the city boy's voice quivered.

"Not spooky, boy." The old man looked at him and winked like before, only with the other eye. "It's midnight, that's all."

The word from the old man's mouth wasn't a word at all. It was a note of music, not some steel-guitar-screeching, three-cord country thing but like something out of one of those city symphonies.

"Ya see, there's somethin' about a rodeo arena at midnight. 'Cause midnight is the time between yesterday and tomorrow with no day of its own. Horses know it. Walk through the buckin' string some night and watch 'em all prickly-eared and head-uppy, some snortin', some pawin' and all of 'em lookin' around. And midnight's something else, too. It's the name of the rankest, meanest, toughest outlaw buckin' horse that ever lived."

The old man's voice faded into that of the announcer. "Next boy out in chute number three is Pete Knight, comes from Crossfield, little north a Calgary. Drawn up on a four-legged whirlwind called Midnight."

And the gate opened, and Cody, who'd been to hundreds of rodeos, and Tom, who'd been to a few, knew. As the spin, the fish-tail, the duck back, the rear and high jump and kick all blended into one, the rider stayed and stayed and spurred. And as he was goin' by the boys, he threw his hat and laughed out loud.

"Only man that ever rode 'im boys. Ol' Pete. Killed a couple of years after by a horse that wasn't half the one you just saw."

Pete was on the ground now, nodding his head to the three of them, and Midnight trotted out along the other side of the fence, glaring at the man and vowing, if a horse can vow, that no man would ever do that again.

"Chute number two and a cowboy from south of the line. The man in the purple chaps, Casey Tibbs, gonna try a bronc called Necklace!" Warren Cooper cried out.

"Watch now, watch," Gabe Pauley touched the boys' shoulders. "Casey won the World five times."

The gate swung open, and the blaze of color that was Casey Tibbs hollered every jump, light like sparks glittering off his spurs, on the horse that sounded like hate, smelled like hate and bucked like hate, not just for this man but for any man in a saddle on his back.

And this time hate won, and the man lost, and the world champion was flailing his way through the air, landing with a whump that sent up dust in puffs that hung in the night air.

"Damn." Gage Pauley drove the toe of a battered boot into the dust. "Thought he could ride 'im."

"So did I," said the man on the ground as he stood and lifted his stetson in salute to the horse that had beaten him. "Howdy, boys, proud to make your acquaintance." The country boy gestured in a way that said he was proud, too, and the city boy nodded. Gabe Pauley had moved down the fence to talk to Casey Tibbs. Tom climbed up alongside his cousin.

"What do you make of all this?" He looked at Cody's shining eyes.

"This? This is the best thing that ever happened to us, to me leastways. Those," he gestured at the waiting infield, "those are my heroes, except instead of bein' in my dreams, they're here." He took hold of Tom's wrist. "They're right here," he repeated through clenched teeth.

"But they're all dead . . ."

Cody nodded and was about to answer when the crackling of the ancient speakers interrupted.

"Next boy out, an Indian boy form the Sarcee reservation. Tom Three Persons is his name. Won the bronc bustin' at the very first Calgary Stampede back in '12, but the horse he's drawn today is twelve hundred pounds of menacing mean. The name of this son-of-a-gun is Five Minutes to Midnight. They're in chute number five. Here we go . . . here we go!"

Even Tom held his breath at the fury of the seconds that followed. The horse did things to throw the cowboy off that neither boy thought possible. Violent, midair contortions, to the left, the right, the left again. Rear up, almost over backward, then down with a motion sure to jerk any cowboy clean out of the saddle.

Except it didn't jerk Tom Three Persons out of the saddle. Not for six seconds, or seven or eight, and then the claxon and, this time both boys cheered and whistled and clapped and stamped. And this time when the cowboy was on the ground and waved, both boys waved back, the city boy's eyes as wide as the boy's from the country.

They looked for Gabe Pauley but couldn't see him and were interrupted by the voice on the loudspeaker again.

"Okay, you fellas, are you ready for a little bull ridin'?" Warren Cooper asked and was answered by a unisoned, "Yeah, you bet!"

"Well, then, look here to chute number one. Brian Claypool of Saskatoon, Saskatchewan, will show you how it's done on a rank bull called Hagar, one of the two or three toughest bulls that ever entered the arena."

"I've heard that name, Brian Claypool," Tom said, his eyes never leaving the chute gate where the young man was settling himself on a furious powder keg about to ignite.

The gate opened and ignite it did, and a violent eight-second ballet began with one partner willing and the other wanting only to be rid of the object, the man on its back. It ended as it began, with the rider in place, dismounting with the aid of a rodeo clown whose face the boys had never seen but had seen a thousand times before.

Brian Claypool raised his arms above his head and grinned a kid grin at the two on the fence, the two who cheered loud enough to be two hundred.

"My dad did the rodeo circuit with him." Cody leaned close to his cousin to tell it. "Brian Claypool and three other cowboys were killed in a plane crash goin' to a rodeo. I think it was a couple of years before I was born."

Then it was Warren Cooper saying, "Okay, boys, a little surprise for ya. Right here at chute number four. Your friend Gabe Pauley on a tough customer called Devastation."

The boys strained to see the figure in chute four who was dwarfed by the massive bull. Head down, hat down so they couldn't see his face. But they did see the head nod, the gate begin to swing open.

And it was over. More suddenly than it had begun. The arena was in darkness again. No sound came over the tired old speakers. The wind could be heard again in the trees to the west and felt on flushed faces.

They waited for a minute, then two, and climbed down from the fence. Silently, each sorting a hundred thoughts, they dust-scuffed their way back to the camper and the lawn chairs they'd been sitting in when the voice of the old cowboy had first broken the night's quiet.

They were still sitting there when Cody's father and some other cowboys came back from telling stories, drinking beer and talking about what they knew, rodeo.

"Still awake, you bandits?" Cody's dad said, his voice a couple of beers louder than usual.

"You . . . you see anything . . . different tonight, Uncle?" Tom asked him.

The men looked at each other, and shrugged and shook their heads and both boys knew they alone had seen.

"Dad, you ever hear of a fella named Gabe Pauley?" Cody looked at the faces of the men as they pulled up chairs and sat down opposite the boys.

"Why you askin', son?"

"No reason. We . . . heard the name tonight," Cody said, his voice a soft night question.

"Gabe Pauley . . ." The men looked around and at the ground and at each other but not at the boys.

"Yeah, Gabe Pauley . . . he was a fella . . . bull rider, he was . . . rode bareback some, too . . . never knew 'im, o' course . . . he was before my time . . . I was probably your age . . . must've been thirty odd years ago . . . in fact, thirty years right on . . . a bull called Devastation . . . killed Gabe Pauley right at this rodeo . . . right over there."

And the city boy and the country boy looked across at the black shadow of the arena that was resting now, gatherin' strength for the next time it would kick up life like dust under a fast horse's hooves."

He finished and I noticed I hadn't yet sipped my coffee. I did then and it was cold. After a few minutes, Jacqueline said, "Have you ever thought of trying to have your work published?"

"Thought of it, yep, I have," Old Jake nodded, "but I prefer to share my stories with my friends. Seems like that's what matters to me."

I stood up. "Sir, I enjoyed your story a great deal. I hope . . . I hope I might do as well one day. I'd like to hear more sometime, I truly would. But if you'll excuse me, I'd like to go for a walk just now."

I nodded to Dad, Jacqueline and February, backed away from the group and the fire, and turned to look into the darkness that seemed to be everywhere else. I didn't know where I was going, but I knew I had to get away from where I'd just been.

Old Jake's story and his way of telling it had taken hold of me the way I so badly wanted my writing to do to others. And here was this little old prune of a man who'd written something that I was pretty sure I'd never equal.

There was more, though. The characters in the story, at least the ones in the phantom rodeo, had been real people. I'd read dozens of journalists' tributes to those men and none had come close to Old Jake's. Like the kid had said, they'd been my heroes and some, my friends. And I wanted to think about them in the best place to do that.

I'd come to the edge of the rodeo arena. I slipped through the rails of the fence and stepped onto the deep soft soil of the infield. No ghosts of long ago here. Just memories. The crew stayed in motels in town so, except for a few bits of equipment and lines of cable, I had the darkened arena to myself. It felt like a good time for some retrospective thinking about my recent decision to retire from rodeo. Not a second guessing session so much as a look back on what had been, to that point, my whole life.

I'd spent at least part of every year for the past thirty-five in rodeo grounds just like this one. I'd slept in them, ate in them, been cheered in several, gored in some, made love in a couple and even delivered a eulogy in one for a friend who'd been killed in a plane crash on the way to one more rodeo, just like in Old Jake's story.

And now it was over. I sat down in the dirt and leaned back on the gate front of chute number five. As I stared up at the Alberta night sky, I found I wasn't thinking of rodeo at all but of Diane, and I wondered if being a cowboy had been worth losing her and Larry.

I'd come to the realization about five years earlier, and ten years too late, that the one thing I really wanted to do well was to raise a family. And sitting there in the dust and electrical cables and cow shit, I realized that of all my failures, and there were a bunch, none was any greater than the failure at being the one thing I'd wanted to be good at.

I watched the Pleiades flicker dim then bright and thought about the time I'd let Diane down most. She was a school secretary, and one day at her school, a retaining wall of some kind had given way during recess. A little girl had been killed and three other kids badly hurt.

When Diane arrived home in a state of near shock, I, of course, wasn't there. I arrived home around midnight in the kind of stupor that was a big part of my life in those days.

As I thought about it, I recognized a sickening parallel between the way Dad had treated Mom and the way I'd treated Diane. As Diane cried and told me what had happened, I tried to put my arms around her. She shrugged me away, something she'd never done before.

And late that night when the roar in my head had reached waterfall proportions, Diane, in a voice as soft as soft is, said, "Dave, I think it's time you and I quit trying to keep something together that wants so badly to come apart."

That's when I made the biggest mistake of my life, before or since. I said, "I guess you're right, Diane."

Above me a meteorite zipped by heading north toward Calgary. I guessed it burned out somewhere over the Stampede grounds. I heard a rustle in the dark, and there was Jacqueline, not saying a word, but sitting down next to me in the dirt like it was something she did all the time.

"You liked the story, didn't you?" she said.

"Naw, the old man can't write shit."

"Yeah."

We sat, both of us with our heads tilted back, watching the stars. "I've just been sitting here wallowing in self-pity and realizing that I've let down every single person who ever counted on me."

"That's not self-pity," Jacqueline said.

"Maybe."

"Your father's counting on you now."

"What, to fight a battle we can't possibly win and one that we're probably not even in the right about?"

"Yes. And whoever said being in the right is all that important anyway?"

"Somebody did. Davy Crockett or Snow White or somebody."

"Can I tell you something . . . something that I think about you?"

"Does it have anything to do with the fact that I'm a terrific guy?"

"Well, not exactly."

"I was afraid of that. More along the lines of 'women hate gutless men'?"

"Somewhere in between."

"Shoot."

"There's something I don't understand. I've heard all the stories about what an off-the-wall guy you are, willing to do weird and wild things at the drop of a hat. I've even seen you that way a few times. And yet when your father, whose behavior is a little . . . odd, I admit, wants to do something eccentric and wonderful, you . . . seem to . . ."

"Look at him like he was something on the bottom of my boot? I think that was the quote."

"Do you like him?"

"Like him?"

"Do you like your father?"

"Jacqueline, I can tell you that for the first forty years of my life with my dad, 'like' never came up. Now, in the last few months, we've suddenly been trying to figure out how we fit into each other's lives . . . I don't know if I like him. I don't think I dislike him."

"He likes you . . . a lot. He's never said it. Maybe never will. But I know he does."

"Look, Jacqueline, about Old Jake. He's a neat old guy, no question. And let's assume for the sake of argument that I want my father and me to be close. Doing something as stupid as what he wants me to do tomorrow isn't going to be what makes the difference. Do you see?"

She began to get up.

"Jacqueline, just a minute, there's something I wanted to ask you the other night but I didn't . . . I guess I didn't feel I should, but I'm curious. You seem like someone who would call herself a feminist. Would you?"

She sat back down but didn't answer for a long time.

"I guess I'd have to say yes," she answered slowly, "though I don't belong to any official group, and I don't generally approve of labels. Why do you ask?"

"I'm not sure," I said. "I'm just trying to sort out some things. I've been asking myself questions."

"What kind of questions?"

"Oh, you know, what would the world be like if the matriarchal system was still in place? What would have happened if the Americans had won the War of 1812? Are Wayne and Janet Gretzky really happy? That sort of thing."

"Why don't you throw in 'Why are we here?'"

"Oh, I dealt with that one when I was still in my teens. I forget the answer just now, but I remember it was brilliant."

"I don't doubt it."

"Then there's another question I'm still wrestling with, which is how you happened to become my stepmother. I know you sort of told me the other night. But you sort of didn't, too."

Jacqueline looked at me. "Do you know what your father said the night he proposed? He said, 'Jacqueline, I want you to know that marrying me doesn't mean giving up one bit of who you are. You'll be free to do whatever you want with the rest of your life. You can write what you want, say what you want, vote the way you want, join Greenpeace if you want' . . . Actually, I think he said 'fucking Greenpeace.' And then he said, 'All I ask is that when I'm sad or I'm sick or happier than a cow knee-deep in green grass, you try to be there to put your arms around me and for me put my arms around you.'"

"My old man said that?"

"Yes, he did and he even told me I could have babies if I wanted to."

"Jesus."

"Of course, he couldn't stand being serious and showing his feelings for too long so he finished of by reminding me that I'm to be his sex slave every Friday night."

We laughed and I shook my head. "The old guy's been doing some things lately that haven't fit in with the way he's lived his life. That speech to you is one of them."

"People change."

"Maybe."

"Anyway, to answer your question, I guess what your father said to me the night he proposed coincides pretty much with my definition of feminism, which is about having the freedom to be the person I want to be. I think with your father I can have that and a hell of a companion besides. I don't think I can say that about any other man I've ever known."

"What about the nights he brings home the Old Jakes of this world?"

"I can handle that. It's really kind of fun. Except that Old Jake snores."

Neither of us said anything for a while. The night felt cool and good, and I liked having her sitting there with me. Then she laughed suddenly and with obvious pleasure.

I looked over at her. "What?"

"Can you keep a secret?"

"I'm a human time capsule."

"I made him get down on his knees."

"To propose?"

"Uh-huh, stark naked. He got out of bed and knelt down beside the bed without a stitch on and actually popped the question."

"You two crazy kids."

"He said he felt foolish."

"I wonder why." We both laughed again and I looked at her. "So what do you plan to do with the rest of your life? Other than on Friday nights, I mean."

"I don't know. Maybe I'll have one of those babies."

"Now I really hope you're kidding."

"There are worse things, you know."

"Name one."

"He didn't do so bad with his first offspring."

I looked back at the sky. "Thanks."

She stood up again. "I'll see you later. Come by for a coffee if you feel like it."

"Goodnight." I watched her go, then looked back up the sky. I tried to spot something I recognized and finally settled on Polaris.

Jacqueline had been gone only a minute or so when it happened.

The thing is, I hadn't "seen" anything in a long while, not since I'd looked down at the sidelines of McMahon Stadium and fallen in love with Ralph. But there it was. As I continued to stare at the North Star, wouldn't you know it, Polaris started to turn into a sort of haze, and the next thing I knew, I was looking into a different dimension. The future, maybe. I wasn't sure at first.

The vision had a fuzzy, dreamlike quality to it, not like most of my clairvoyant experiences. It was like looking at a television with the fine-tuning out of whack. Maybe this particular vision was supposed to be symbolic. Anyway, there I was dressed in U.S. cavalry blues, sword raised, looking around at my men and leading them down a hill in the standard television cavalry charge.

What we were charging at wasn't clear. That was left to me to figure out.

It didn't take a lot of figuring. "Shit, that hill's gotta be overlooking Old Jake's place. I'm supposed to get a bunch of people together to chase off the bad guys."

There was an immediate problem. It was nine-thirty at night. Dad had said the sheriff would be coming at four o'clock the next afternoon. That didn't give me a lot of time to organize a cavalry raid a couple hundred miles south of here in a foreign country. Where damn near everybody carries a gun.

"Fucking perfect," I told Polaris as it returned to focus. "Thanks a lot."

One thing I didn't do was argue with the things I saw. The vision said I was leading the cavalry; it was up to me to lead the goddamn cavalry. Of course, the vision didn't bother to explain how that was supposed to happen. Come to think of it, there hadn't been a lot of directions supplied for winning over Angela either.

I ran for a telephone. Normally, it's preferable to recruit soldiers in person, but there wasn't time for that. My first call was to Doug. If he was sober, I knew he'd love the idea. Doug loves all wacky ideas. My fear was that the cavalry might consist of Doug and me.

He answered. "Hello."

"Doug, it's me, Doc. I don't have a lot of time to explain. Can you ride a horse?"

"No."

"Perfect. I need you to be at the Havre Rodeo grounds tomorrow at noon.

"Havre?"

"Yeah."

"Havre, Montana?"

"Yeah. I worked a rodeo there six or seven years ago. You went along with me, remember?"

"I know where the fucking place is."

"Good, then there shouldn't be a problem."

"Hey, listen, Dana is here and we're sort of busy, you know. I don't think I can make it."

"Doug, you'll love this gig. It's a confrontation with authority. You enjoy that shit."

"Not in the U.S. of A. pal. They shoot people just for laughs down there."

"I'm serious. I need this favor. Be there, will you?"

I hung up not knowing for certain whether my army had doubled in number or not. A lot would depend on how the rest of Doug's night went. Either way, I wasn't confident. He'd either be pissed off or exhausted.

I phoned Tub Willoughby.

"Tub, I'm looking for a favor."

"Name it, buddy."

"I need you to get on the blower to some of the people we know in rodeo, as many as you can. Get 'em to the Havre Rodeo grounds by noon tomorrow. They have to bring their own horses and tack, and if anybody can bring extra horses, we can use them."

"Fourteen hours from now, huh? Sounds like a piece of goddamn cake. Wanna tell me what it's about?"

"No time. I'll explain tomorrow. See ya Tub, and thanks."

I was counting on the fact that one of the unique aspects of rodeo life is that those of us in it really do consider ourselves, in the words of the cliché, "one big family." Notice I don't include the word "happy," mostly because it doesn't apply. That's because one of the more unfortunate characteristics of the rodeo community is that there are those who believe that be considered truly tough—surely a prerequisite for being a cowboy—you can't be doing a lot of smiling.

Nevertheless, when the call for help goes out, my experience is that you can count on cowboys to answer. Cowgirls, too, for that matter. Though I'm not sure why, since barrel racers are often treated as rather less than equals in the male-dominated world of rodeo. Still, I knew they'd be there if they could. Of course, one usually allows for more lead time than I was giving, but that couldn't be helped.

I also called Reverend Hobnatz in the hope that he might know how to reach the rugby guys from the wedding. He said he'd do what he could. At least I think that's what he said. He sounded . . . well . . . stoned, but maybe it was just a bad phone connection.

The next bit of recruiting couldn't be done over the phone. So I climbed into the GMC and set out to find the camp of the Satan's Halos. I was taking a chance. I didn't want the banker killed or even roughed up, just encouraged to leave. Still, I figured the Halos' presence would add a certain dimension to our little force that few others could. There's nothing like good old-fashioned intimidation to change people's attitudes.

I found the Halos' camp after about an hour and a half of driving. I had arrived in the middle of a party. Of course, I'm not sure I could have arrived at a time that wasn't in the middle of a party. It took quite a while to find Suzy, the problem being—and I know I'm stereotyping again—that the Halos all look alike.

After turning down a lot of beer and a couple of proposals that involved tongues and breasts, I found Suzy relaxing in a makeshift jacuzzi. It was a giant stock water trough with a hose running into it. The other end of the hose was attached to the exhaust pipe of a Harley. The bike's single cylinder popped away, quite adequately providing a function that I doubt Messrs. Harley and Davidson had ever envisaged.

Suzy was flanked by a pair of bare-chested women who gave every indication that their nakedness extended to areas below their respective bosoms. As badly as I wanted to get out of there, I thought it wise to take a little more time with my explanation to Suzy of what was needed. He listened. I think it was listening; his head was back and rolling around like he was trying to get a kink out of his neck.

I finished my explanation, but the only reaction I got was more of the head rolling. Then Suzy looked at me. His eyes were open very wide, as if he were seeing me for the first time. Or preparing to belch.

"Sounds interesting," he said. "Your friend gonna be there, the crazy bastard ball player?"

I was puzzled for a minute since that description could have applied to almost anyone on the team. "You mean Doug? The guy who hit the home . . . the triple in the game against you guys."

"The guy I was going to exterminate."

"Oh, that crazy bastard ball player. Uh . . . yeah . . . he might be part of our group. Is that going to be a prob—"

"I like that son-of-a-bitch," Suzy said, then belched, the wide eyes apparently having had a two-fold purpose.

"Yeah, Doug's a likable son-of-a-bitch, all right." I wondered what fate worse than extermination might have been planned for Doug had Suzy not liked him.

"'Course I can't guarantee anything. We have to talk it over. This is a democratic society here." He put his arms around his two companions to illustrate his point.

"Uh-huh, well that's fair." I took Suzy's statement to mean that Wink would have to be consulted.

"So get in and explain it to me again so I got the facts right."

"Get in? There?" I wondered what chemical reaction carbon monoxide and water mixed in this innovative way might produce.

"Yeah. Oh, I get it. You haven't met the girls yet. This is Liz and this is Flo."

Liz said hi and Flo grinned, which showed the inside of her mouth, definitely not her best feature because about half of her teeth, including some critical ones from an aesthetic point of view, were no longer there.

"Geez, I'd like to, but I've got some more organizing to do on this thing. We'll damn sure do it another time, though." I began to back up slowly, the way I always figured I would if confronted by a pack of crazed wolves.

"Get in." It was more than an invitation but less than an order. Nevertheless, I got the impression that Suzy wouldn't take kindly to my continued refusal of his hospitality.

I started to climb in. Suzy frowned and made a face that said it's gauche to get in the water with your clothes on.

I clumsily began unbuckling my belt, secure in the knowledge that the chill of the night air and the combined stare of Liz and Flo, whose gaze was riveted on my lower abdomen, had shrunk my manhood to the size of a lentil.

CHAPTER TWELVE

The next day—the details of what took place in and out of the jacuzzi and my subsequent escape shall remain forever untold—I found myself in the middle of the damnedest array of strange characters ever assembled for military action.

The media came to call the event "The Great Coyote Creek Charge for Freedom of Nineteen and Eighty-nine." You probably heard about it. It was written up in lots of books. There's likely something on the subject in your local library. Somebody even wrote a poem about it, and Ian Tyson recorded a song that did pretty well on the country charts. I can't say I was crazy about the name they hung on the event, mostly because there isn't a place called Coyote Creek within a two day ride of Old Jake's place, and the thing didn't happen in nineteen eighty-nine. But the media folks, especially Dan Rather, seemed to like the sound of the name so none of us made much fuss over a couple of minor inaccuracies.

Old Jake's place was situated in a pretty little valley about a half mile southwest of Havre. The area is cattle country, cowboy country—working cowboys, not the rodeo variety—populated by a breed of people not generally given to being shocked by unusual sights.

Nevertheless, those who saw us as we made our way toward Old Jake's through the hills that surround the place on three sides expressed considerable shock and more than a little dismay. As we came to a halt on the other side of the hill closest to Old Jake's house, I had a chance to really look at the force I'd mustered. We were a solid line that stretched a couple football fields wide. At least that's how I think we would have looked had we overcome a certain lack of discipline in our ranks and actually formed a line.

Larry was next to me on my right, and for a kid who thought he'd outgrown rodeo, he seemed to be enjoying the outlaw side of the Wild West. He was dressed like a miniature member of the Hole in the Wall gang. Next to Larry was Tub Willoughby and next to him, Stan Shofner. I'd been a little shocked when Stan showed up, but to put things in perspective, his greeting to me had been "Okay, chickenshit. I'm here. This better be awful fuckin' good."

After Stan came a fair representation of cowboys—my faith in the rodeo fraternity having been justified—ropers, doggers, bronc and bull riders, and a couple of rodeo rookies I'd never even met. On my left was Rhonda Rae Crockett and behind her, riding double, and doing a lot of clinging and whining was Doug. He was scared to death of horses so the clinging seemed desperate and had little to do with the fact that he was perched behind one of the better backsides in the sport of rodeo. A solid contingent of barrel racers were on the other side of Rhonda Rae, and beyond them were several members of the Kingsland Rugby squad.

We had run out of horses, but that hadn't deterred the rugby types. Several were riding mountain bikes, and the rest had scrounged quads, trikes, skateboards and other wheeled vehicles I'd never seen before. Seems Old Jake's neighbors were tickled to help the infiltrators from the north. I had a nagging feeling they were just looking forward to seeing us all get shot. My only disappointment was that the Halos were not represented in the group. I assumed either that Suzy had been outvoted or that the party was still ongoing.

Reverend Hobnatz rode over to me as we counted down the last few minutes to four o'clock. He was mounted—smaller minds than mine might say fittingly—on an unhappy looking donkey.

"Requesting permission to lead the troops in a prayer, sir," he said as he flailed away at the donkey's sides with the heels of his Reeboks.

"Why not," I said. "We might need it."

After what seemed like an eternity, Reverend Hobnatz was able to get the uncooperative beast turned and facing the faithful.

"Bow your heads, please!" he cried in a voice that rolled through, over and around the hills.

"Can you keep it down a little?" I hissed at him.

"The Lord's voice knows no volume control." He raised a hand in the air.

I eased my horse over next to the donkey. "If you don't pray quietly, I'll have that donkey do some things to your body that will bring new meaning to the word martyr."

Reverend Hobnatz regarded me as one does a sinner with no hope of salvation. "I understand." He faced the group once more. "Dearly beloved," he began at a much more acceptable level, "we are gathered here to . . ."

He looked over at me, "Why are we gathered here?"

"He missed the meeting," Larry explained.

I looked at my watch. "Just bless 'em. We gotta go."

"I can't bless 'em if you don't bow your head."

"There's never a lion around when you need one," Doug said.

I bowed my head.

We didn't receive the full benefit of the Reverend's supplication, however, as his voice was drowned out by the arrival of a noise of much greater proportion. I un-bowed my head and opened my eyes. Approaching from behind us was the roar of many engines. Loud engines. Harley Davidson engines. At least two dozen members of the

Satan's Halos, some with their women behind them, were coming up the hill, revving motors as only motorcycle riders can rev. They were moving slowly, very slowly. Out of necessity. Because on the two flanks of the line of bikers came Suzy and Wink, not on bikes but at the controls of two D-6 caterpillars.

Reverend Hobnatz leaned toward me and pointed at the reinforcements. "The power of prayer," he said.

When we reached the top of the hill, I looked down at the scene below. The guy I took to be the banker and three other guys, official looking types in uniforms, were standing at the gate leading into the yard around Old Jake's house.

On the other side of the gate stood Old Jake, February, my father and Jacqueline. It occurred to me that four on four is a fair fight, and I briefly considered calling the whole thing off. Two things kept me from doing that. The first was the realization that the four people on the outside of the gate had the power of the state behind them, which tipped the scales rather dramatically in the banker's favor. The second reason was that I wasn't convinced about the wisdom of telling the likes of Stan Shofner and Wink and Suzy that I'd changed my mind and that they could take their means of transportation back to wherever the hell they'd gotten them from.

The scene in the yard below went into tableau. Eight pairs of eyes turned to watch our very noisy advance down the slope to Old Jake's place. Not one of the people in the yard spoke or moved, other than the banker whose mouth opened wider the closer we came.

A barbed wire fence separated us from the yard itself, and I held up my hand, cowboy movie style, to bring my troop to a halt just the other side of the fence.

"Morning, son," my dad spoke first. "Glad you decided to drop by."

Jacqueline had tears in her eyes, and I could be wrong, but I thought there might've been a little glistening around the banker's cheekbones, too, for a different reason, of course.

"Doc Allen, I'd like you to meet Mr. Hempworth." Old Jake made the introduction. "Mr. Hempworth is with the bank. These other gentlemen are the sheriff and two bailiffs Mr. Hempworth brought along to see to it that I get off my land. Mr. Hempworth, meet Doc Allen."

I tipped my hat to the banker who had finally got his mouth to close. "Sir, my friends and I came by this morning to see if we couldn't persuade you to pursue another course of action."

"I won't be threatened by a show of force, Mr. Allen, and I remind you that should you choose to obstruct due process of the law, you will face serious legal consequences.

"The guy's a dickhead," Doug said loud enough for everyone in the yard to hear.

"Let's kick some ass," Stan Shofner said.

"Quit the bullshit. I wanna have some fun," Suzy yelled, and this was followed by a crescendo of Harley-Davidson engine noise.

When it died down, I spoke again. "Mr. Hempworth, I'm not sure how long I can keep these people back because they feel strongly that what you're doing to Mr. Bowlen and his son is wrong. So what I'd suggest is that I count to five, and you fellas move along before I finish."

"You can't get away with this," Hempworth blustered.

"One," I said.

The sheriff and his bailiffs were beginning to look uncomfortable. I couldn't tell if they had guns or not, but my guess was that they had.

"Two."

"Sheriff Marsden, call for help at once. I refuse to allow the bank to be bullied by these . . . hooligans." This brought another roar from the Harleys. Apparently, you can call a biker a fat-ass dip-shit and earn his respect, but he doesn't take kindly to being called a hooligan.

"Three."

The sheriff and his men had begun to drift toward their car. To his credit, Hempworth, much braver than he was smart, stood his ground.

"This is an outrage, an absolute—"

"Four."

The sheriff and bailiffs got into the car.

The banker turned to Old Jake. "Mr. Bowlen, this will not go well with you if you allow this . . . indecency to take place on your property."

"Make up your mind," Old Jake shrugged. "I thought it was your property, which is why you want me to get off. Now if we agree that it's my property, then I'm sure . . ."

"We most certainly do not agree . . ."

That was as far as he got because at that point Suzy and Wink throttled the cats into action and instantly created a pair of large holes in the fence. The group divided and poured through the improvised entrances into Old Jake's yard, leaving me alone on the other side of what was left of the fence.

"Five," I said to myself.

The sheriff's car spun considerable gravel as the three men made a rapid exit from the scene of the action.

Hempworth had not moved, and I could just hear his high-pitched voice over the deafening racket that was everywhere.

"Do not, I warn you, harm so much as a twenty-five cent piece worth of bank property, or I assure you, you will rue the blackness of your deeds."

Somehow Wink and Suzy figured out that the car remaining in the yard, a spotlessly clean, blue Lebaron must have been Hempworth's company car. The two caterpillars, blades down, approached each other slowly, relentlessly, like first daters bent on a goodnight kiss. Between them was bank property valued at considerably more than a twenty-five cent piece.

The sound a car makes as it's being scrunched into the width of a clubhouse sandwich is quite unforgettable. In fact, everyone stopped what they were doing, which was mostly riding around "ki-yi"ing to beat hell, like you see in the old westerns, and watched in fascinated silence. The car, I figured it for about twenty grand worth, folded up like a styrofoam cup. Mr. Hempworth's mouth once again assumed the open position.

Suzy and Wink's handiwork completed, the whole thing was over except for the cleanup. Hempworth, realizing at last that he was not dealing with reasonable people, picked up the briefcase he'd had beside him the whole time and began walking away from the yard. He had to deviate from a straight line to go around horses, strewn fence and what remained of his car.

"The body shop guys are doing really great work these days," Wink said from the seat of his Cat as Hempworth went by. "They'll have you back behind the wheel in a couple of days tops."

I rode into the yard then, and Hempworth looked at me, eyes blank. This was clearly not a scenario they had prepared him for at bank school, and I felt a little sorry for him.

"You are a lunatic," he said. "A complete raving madman."

"Yeah," I smiled and looked around. "Hey, I need a volunteer to run Mr. Hempworth here back to town. Anybody?"

"We will." I turned, and there were Liz and Flo commandeering a bike from one of the Halos.

They roared up alongside Hempworth who, after apparently weighing his options, climbed up behind Liz with as much dignity as the situation would permit. Flo climbed on behind Hempworth and waved as they roared off down the road. I had the feeling that the banker would have more to talk about when he got back to the office than a crushed Chrysler.

It was time to celebrate. I learned quickly that the one common thread binding my eclectic group of warriors together was an ability to have a party anywhere, anytime with minimal preparation. This, of course, was facilitated by the fact that, as always, the Halos had brought along enough beer to supply our own little army and three or four more like it. In less than an hour, the fence had been repaired, the vehicles were all lined up in orderly fashion, and the participants in The Great Coyote Creek Charge for Freedom of Nineteen and Eighty-nine were well on their way to enjoying victory stupors.

I wandered up onto the porch of the tiny house Old Jake and his son lived in. I wondered why the authorities could possibly want it. Dad and

Jacqueline were sitting side by side in rocking chairs. They were holding hands and smiling.

"We showed 'em, didn't we. For once the little guy won," Dad said.

It was one of the rare occasions in my life that I didn't feel like arguing with my father. "Yeah, Dad, we showed 'em. The little guy won."

"Did I ever tell you I'm damn glad you're my kid?"

"Well, not actually, but you were probably busy and—"

"I should have." He stood up then. "I should have, a hell of a long time ago."

"Thanks, Dad."

"Here, sit down, visit with Jacqueline. I better go help Old Jake. Last time I saw him, he was trying to figure out how to make chip dip. I don't think they have a lot of parties here."

Suzy strolled by the porch. "Hey, see if they got any music around here. We feel like dancin'."

"Music coming up," Dad waved and moved off. I sat down in the rocker.

Jacqueline looked at me and smiled. "He's really proud of you."

"I'm glad. Maybe he'll come and see me in jail."

Suzy leaned over the railing of the old porch and handed me a beer. "You were right. This was shittin' great. Next year, you guys, us, another ball game, huh?"

"A shittin' great idea, Suzy," I said.

"Yo! I'll go tell my man, Doug." Suzy waved a clenched fist and headed off to spread the good news.

I leaned my head back on the rocker, feeling suddenly very tired. "I may have to get one of these," I said.

"You know, you'll never be able to say that again." Jacqueline put her hand on my arm.

"What, that I want a rocking chair?"

"No, that thing about how you've let everyone down who ever counted on you."

"What? This? This wasn't much."

"Yes it was. It was a very big thing to those two old men."

I didn't try to answer.

"Now, why don't you do something for yourself?'

"What do you suggest, Jacqueline?"

"Why don't you go get your woman back?"

"Can't be done. Believe me, I've tried. The lady knows what she wants in her life and I'm not it."

"I can't believe that the guy who put all this together today can't think of a way to persuade a woman that he's the man for her."

"Sorry to disappoint but—"

"So that's it then. You're just giving up."

"I'm not giving up. I'm facing reality."

"While the woman you love leaves town with the worst defensive back in CFL history?"

"I hate to hear it put in those words, but yeah . . . I guess."

"Don't you think it would be worth one last try?"

"Even if I did, I wouldn't know where to find her."

"Especially if you don't look."

"You're not making this easy."

"That's the idea."

"I've got to finish the work I was doing on the script. She'll be gone in a few days. I'll be too late."

"So we work on the script together. I bet we could finish it today. That gives you at least a little time to find her and make her fall madly in love with you. Larry can stay with us for a few days."

"Sounds easy as hell."

"Come on, let's go. I'll tell your father we're leaving. You say good-bye to them," she waved her arm, "and we go to work."

"You know, of course, that there isn't a chance this is going to work."

"There wasn't a chance that this," she waved again, "would work either."

Dad stuck his head out the window. "I found some music. All we got is a record player that's older than dirt, but here it is."

Dad propped the record player up next to the open window and turned the volume up as loud as it would go on the ancient instrument. I don't think the music was what Suzy had in mind for dancing, but as I listened to the scratchy rhythms coming from the player, I figured maybe that wasn't the point.

I didn't recognize the singer, but I knew the song right off.

O give me land lots of land
Under starry skies above
Don't fence me in.
Let me ride over wide
Open country that I love
Don't fence me in.
Let me be by myself in the evening breeze,
Listen to the murmur of the Cottonwood trees,
Send me off forever but I ask you please
Don't fence me in.
Just turn me loose
Let me wander over yonder . . .

CHAPTER THIRTEEN

Jacqueline was right about the first part at least. We got the script done that afternoon. A lot of it was mine, too. She said it was pretty good. And late that night, I was back in Calgary, a city of six hundred thousand or so trying to find the girl who'd made me love Ralph the Dog.

I had a plan.

When I got back to the city, I went straight to Doug's place, packed my sleeping bag, shaving kit, a bag of oranges and a carton of oreo cookies and headed for the airport. I decided to take a cab, and eighteen dollars later, I entered the terminal and set up camp in what I figured was a strategic place to see most departing passengers.

I knew that a major obstacle in my plan was going to be airport security so I decided to deal with it immediately. I faked an accent and told a uniformed guy who looked moderately friendly that, "I am no having any more money, and my air-o-craft is leaving not for three days back to . . . to Bucharest . . . please may I stay quietly out of the way in this little corner by this machinery?"

Actually, it was one of those machines you could buy flight insurance from. The security guy bought my story and even lent me five bucks to get something to eat. I felt bad taking the guy's money but not bad enough to turn it down. For the next couple of hours, I toured all the airline counters until I had a pretty good idea of every possible flight Angela could take to get to Dayton.

My plan was simple, yet ingenious. Assuming that she didn't somehow slip past me, I was going to stay in the airport until she came to get on her flight, a matter of a few days, a week at the most. I would wait until she was actually in the ticket lineup, then jump on her, wrestle her to the floor and threaten to expose her as a Columbian drug lord if she didn't agree to spend the next thirty years helping me pay off a mortgage.

Several times I tried to get the ol' psychic powers to kick in, just to give me a little preview of how things might turn out, but no go. One of the things I like least about the whole psychic thing is that it seems to start and stop whenever it damn well feels like, with almost no regard for my needs.

The hours spent sitting in my little corner of the terminal at Calgary International did give me time to develop some doubts about the plan. But I was unable to come up with a better idea and turned my attention to other time-consuming pursuits. I began writing a short story about a rodeo clown who is murdered by an unscrupulous calf roper. But before he dies, the clown puts a curse on the calf-roping event, and for the next ten years, no calf is ever roped at the Calgary Stampede. I figured the story would be a big hit with the animal rights people.

I met some interesting folks, too. I had quite a row with a large cartoon character of a woman from Albany, New York, who was inserting money into one of the insurance machines. I tried to explain to her that the whole life insurance business is a scam. I eventually had to back down when the friendly security agent—by then I'd learned his name was Martin—came over to see what was going on, and I couldn't see myself pursuing the argument with my fake Rumanian accent.

I discovered other interesting types among the human flotsam that populates the departure level of an airport. A couple of gays from San Francisco bought me lunch, and I spent an absorbing hour with them as they tried to persuade me that maybe their lifestyle was the solution to the turmoil in my own life. They gave me their address, and I told them maybe Angela and I would drop in on them sometime.

A television evangelist from South Carolina became keenly interested when I told him I was heir to the Canadian Tire millions and had a sister with forty-inch buzooms, and that she liked to do kinky things with tartar sauce.

I also met a kick boxer from Trois-Rivieres who showed me a couple of useful moves if the security guy should turn ugly, a Revenue Canada bureaucrat who told me to get a fucking job and a woman who I was absolutely convinced was Meryl Streep but who told me her name was Lois Barker.

And there was Angela.

The third day of my vigil, I saw her. She was in the American Airlines ticket line. My heart began to beat at about the same rate it had the first time I faced a bull named Crooked Nose who had a reputation for remodeling clowns' bodies to make them look like Picasso portraits.

For a few minutes, I was honestly frozen in place. At the exact moment I saw her, I was sitting on my rolled-up sleeping bag, a Saul Bellows novel in one hand, a bag of Jumbo Crunchits in the other and my walkman on my head. Stevie Wonder was suggesting that "Ba–bay, everything is all right, uptight, outta sight." I wasn't so sure except for the uptight part, which is what I was, big time.

Angela purchased her ticket and began walking right toward me, her face in that detached, senses-shut-off glaze that airport terminals inspire in people. She was practically beside me and hadn't seen me yet.

"Crunchit?" I held out the bag.

For a few seconds she looked at me without saying anything. Then I saw her lips move.

I took off the headphones. "What?"

"I said, how long have you been waiting?"

"Most of my adult life."

"What are you doing here?" She set down her carry-on bag, which I felt was definite grounds for optimism. "And don't say something stupid."

"Actually, I was planning our life together." I hoped that wasn't stupid.

"I hope you don't think you're getting on that plane with me."

I saw Martin, the security guard, lurking a few feet behind her.

"No, I am no thinking theese," I said, "though eese no bad idea."

"Why are you talking like that?"

Martin moved off.

"Like what?" I shrugged.

"Geez, you can piss a person off." She picked up her bag.

This was not time to piss her off. I stood up. "Actually, I was hoping I could stop you from getting on that aircraft." My three days in the airport had taught me that people in the business call them aircraft.

"How were you planning to do that?" She began walking toward her departure gate.

"I'm not sure," I admitted. "I haven't ruled out throwing myself under the wheels. By the way, where's Patty?"

"She's staying with my mother for a while to give Dennis and me a chance to . . . Why am I explaining anything to you? And besides, we've been through this," she said, picking up the pace a little. "It's been decided."

"Not really," I said. "You voted for, I voted against. That's a tie. In Canada that means we have to send it to committee for study."

She stopped. I stopped. She looked at me as if to suggest either pity or tenderness. I chose tenderness.

"I'm sorry, Dave . . . Doc. I really am. I believe that you care for me. And I like you. But that isn't enough, you see?"

We started walking again, pretty fast this time.

"It is enough, to start with," I argued-pleaded-whined. "We build on it from there. I spoil you rotten, and in two years we're sitting on the porch of our little place in the country, listening to the frogs and the coyotes and the far-off train whistle, and you turn to me and say, 'Y'know, you big handsome lug, you were right all along. This really is paradise. Now let's go in the house and make a baby.'"

We were at the security walk-through. She showed the attendant her ticket.

"I'm going now, Dave." She kissed me on the cheek, a major come-down from her previous goodbye offering.

I started into the walk-through after her. A guard stopped me.

Angela beeped on her way through and was being checked over by a female security guard on the other side. On my side, the guard, a thoroughly humorless and very large guy, was obviously willing to lay down his life to keep me out of there.

"This is your big chance for happiness. You're throwing it away," I called out.

Angela looked back for about a millisecond after they'd finished checking her over with the metal detector thing and then began moving toward Departure Gates 22 – 26. I don't know if it was watching her disappear into the knot of passengers going away from me or the frustration of being held in a bear hug by a security guard with breath that bordered on being a criminal offense.

Anyway, I snapped. "Yeah, well go!" I screamed. "I don't need you, you know. I was getting along just fine before you came into my life, wiggling your butt around in a stupid dog costume."

I was hollering and crying and pounding a fist against my leg. The security guard let me go.

I continued to shout, even though I could no longer see Angela. "I'm going to sit on the porch of that place in the country beside an empty chair and be just fine, thanks, without you."

I started walking away and then turned back for a final salvo. "And you were a horseshit Ralph the Dog, too!" I called to the now empty security area.

I turned again and this time made my way back to where I'd left my stuff. Martin was standing there.

"You okay?" he said.

"Yeah, I'm fine," I answered. "Can I ask you something? Is there something fundamentally wrong with me?"

"Naw," Martin shook his head. "I mean, you desperately need a shave and you could use a bath and your European accent was crap. But other than that, you're all right."

I bent over and began packing up my gear. "When did you figure out the accent was phony?"

"About halfway through your first sentence."

I nodded. I was having trouble getting things organized because there were tears in my eyes and everything looked blurry.

"You think I could maybe get a job here in security?" I asked him. "I'm good with people."

"I noticed that," Martin said.

"I don't know." I shoved Saul Bellow into my backpack. "Maybe I'll go back to school or something. Computers might be the way to go. Lots of money in computers. You know much about computers, Martin?"

He didn't answer and I looked up. Martin was gone.

Angela was standing where he'd been.

"I didn't think I was that bad," she said.

I blinked but couldn't, for one of the few times in my life, make my mouth work.

"As Ralph," she took a step toward me. "I didn't think I was as bad as you said."

"You were great," I whispered.

"You better be as good to me as you said." She put the carry-on bag down and knelt down with me.

I nodded. For some reason, there were more tears in my eyes now, and I wiped my nose on my sleeve.

Angela put her arms around me. "And don't ever call me 'the woman.'"

As Angela put the softest cheek I've ever known against mine, I saw Martin over her shoulder. He was grinning so hard his face had to be hurting.

And the airport security guard and I pantomimed a long distance high-five that had nothing to do with winning and everything to do with victory.